GREAT RECKONING

GREAT
RECKONING

by NANCY FAULKNER

E. P. DUTTON & CO., INC.   NEW YORK

Published simultaneously in Canada by Clarke,
Irwin & Company Limited, Toronto and Vancouver

SBN: 0-525-30997-7 (Trade)   SBN: 0-525-30998-5
Library of Congress Catalog Card Number: 71-116882
Designed by Hilda Scott
Printed in the U.S.A.
First Edition

For
Elizabeth F. Gresham

Contents

When a man's verses cannot be understood, nor a man's good wit seconded with the forward child Understanding, it strikes a man more dead than a great reckoning in a little room.

As You Like It
Act III, scene iii

CHAPTER I

An End and a Beginning

"Hurry! Hurry! Hurry!"

Dickon Fontayne stood in the stableyard of Old Hobson's posting house in Cambridge and said the words silently, willing the stable lads to speed. He wanted to shout aloud—and was afraid. He wanted to go himself into the stable and find a swift horse and ride pell-mell all the way to Chipping Norton and Tom—and did not dare.

If he made one wrong move he would surely call attention to himself and, more than likely, bring upon his head the scorn of the three or four men waiting patiently enough for horses. And once he had seen in another's eyes the realization of his stupidity and fecklessness, his inability to cope with the ordinary problems of getting a horse and beginning a journey, he would destroy the brittle surface calm he had succeeded in laying upon his mind.

One of the boys brought out a starveling nag and

led it to a waiting man. The man groaned and swore. "By all the saints," he said, "what *is* this? You can't expect me to ride that—that broken-down hobbyhorse! Bring me a decent mount, and quickly."

The boy turned away and went back toward the stable, not bothering to answer. Another of the men in the yard laughed a short, explosive snort. "It's plain you've not relied upon our Hobson before," he said. "Hobson's rules are unbreakable. You take the horse nearest the door or none."

The stranger looked at him as if he'd lost his wits. "Bu—but that—that's nonsense," he said.

"No. Old Hobson's got a fondness for animals, you see. The horse nearest the door is the most rested in the stables. So that one goes first. 'Hobson's choice' we call it in these parts. Which is to say, there's no choice at all."

Dickon grinned at the rider's discomfort as he mounted the poor beast, shaking his head all the time. But the grin soon faded and Dickon began to pace the yard as if his quick, jerky movements would put speed into the leaden feet of the attendants.

Now and again he looked over his shoulder at the squat towers and soaring spires that marked out the colleges of Cambridge University against the brightening sky of early day. This had been his home for five years, since the time he was ten and his father newly dead of wounds taken in Armada fight, and Tom Fontayne brought his young brother to Queen's College.

Dickon hadn't wanted to come. He had begged and pleaded to be allowed to stay at home; to roam as he chose about the wide fields and pastures of his father's lands; to hunt for hares in the deep oak woods and fish the streams that ran through the estate. But, for once, Tom refused to spoil him. The master of the grammar school, Tom said, thought Dickon a clever lad and for clever lads the place to be was the university, not growing up like a bumpkin without knowing any of the things a proper gentleman should know. So Tom took Dickon to his own old college and left him there, except for brief vacations when their serving man, Peter Farmer, came to bring him safely home for a while.

Dickon bit down hard upon his lower lip. He didn't *want* to leave Cambridge. He loved the ordered, quiet life of the university. Even as a small boy of ten he had come quickly to know that studying under learned men satisfied some need of his spirit he'd never guessed, there at Chipping Norton, existed. Each year, each day, his satisfaction in acquiring knowledge had grown until he had hardly noticed these last two years when Tom had not sent for him at vacation time. Over and over in these years he had been reminded of the words of the poet Chaucer, "the life so short, the craft so long to learn," and he had grudged each hour away from his books. He had hoped to spend the rest of his days here at Cambridge as a scholar teaching other boys the joys of learning.

But now. . . . Now he was sent for. Tom was sick and needed him at home to help with the land. And what did *he* know about caring for property, about raising sheep and selling the wool, about dealing with men of the law and attending to the myriad problems of running a great estate? The very thought of such things terrified him. He no longer even thought of Chipping Norton as home. This—this sanctuary of the mind—this was his home.

When the master of the college had called him yesterday, and had showed him the letter from Tom, Dickon had been too stunned to think properly. He could do nothing but wonder about the long journey ahead of him and he had asked, "Where is Peter, then?"

"Peter?" the master repeated as if he were bemused.

"Peter Farmer who always comes to see me safely home," Dickon explained, the words coming dully from his dulled mind.

"Richard Fontayne!" The master shouted the words, using Dickon's proper name for the first time in many months. "Richard Fontayne, you are fifteen years old and a Bachelor of Arts at Queen's College. Let me hear no more talk of your being seen safely home by some servant of your house. That is for new boys, not for a man near grown and entitled to be called Master. You'll see yourself home and quickly. Your brother needs you." He looked at Dickon's miserable face and added more gently. "But when Tom is well again, come back to us. There will always be a place here for so sharp a scholar."

So here he was, torn between misery at leaving Cambridge and fear for the journey he must make for the first time alone. And there was another misery, too. For, during the long night while he lay upon his bed, waiting for dawnlight, the full meaning of Tom's letter had thrust itself at him. Tom must be very ill indeed to bring him away from those studies his brother set such store by.

He kicked the bundle of belongings at his feet as if it were Tom's illness and he could kick it away. Why didn't the boy come with the horse so he could get quickly home and nurse Tom to health again and so come back to what he loved most in all the world?

"Are you Master Dickon Fontayne?"

Dickon whirled about to the voice and saw a boy holding a sleek black mare.

"You're lucky," the boy said, grinning. "This one's a fine beast and fast."

Dickon nodded and gave the boy a farthing for his trouble, hoping it was enough. He took the reins and ran his hands over the horse and knew she was, indeed, a fine animal. With luck he could be at Chipping Norton in no more than three days.

And pray heaven, when he came there, he'd find Tom mending and all this pother a useless waste of time. If he didn't, if Tom were really as ill as he thought himself, if Dickon Fontayne were to be held for endless days wrestling with things he knew nothing of, what then? He shuddered and tried to put the thoughts away from him and mounted his horse and rode out of Hobson's yard.

"Please, Tom. Have a care!"

Dickon, sitting beside the great carved bed where his brother lay, put a quieting hand on Tom's shoulders as he tried to sit up.

"The—devil—take—this—weakness," Tom panted. He rested a minute. Dickon, still dismayed by the thin body and the drawn, exhausted face with its two spots of brilliant color, watched him. After the pause Tom spoke more strongly.

"Better now." His emaciated hands moved restlessly on the thick coverlet that seemed to weigh too heavily for his strength. Dickon reached to draw it back but Tom stopped him. "Leave it, Dickon. Cold without it. Listen well now. There are things you must know and a boon you must grant me."

"Let it wait awhile, Tom," Dickon said.

He had come at midday to the stone house of many windows and rich furnishings that had been his father's pride in the days when his mother had walked its rooms with grace and love. He had found Tom, burning with fever and fretful with pain the physician had been unable to relieve with his leeches and his plasters. The shock of finding his brother so much worse than he had expected was still upon Dickon, and he felt lost and frightened. His only sensible thought was to keep Tom quiet, but Tom did not want it so.

"Dickon, Dickon," Tom said, and coughed as if he would never stop. "You *must* hear me out. Now."

Tom stopped to gather his breath and Dickon waited. Something in this strange illness seemed to force his brother to speech as hectic as the fever flush upon his face. Dickon smoothed the rumpled pillow under Tom's head and said, trying to speak lightly, "Surely these things can wait until you're well again."

Tom's thin hand gripped his wrist and held on fiercely. Dickon wondered where his brother got his more-than-human strength.

"There is no time, Dickon," Tom said, and Dickon felt his spine prickle at the desperation in his brother's voice.

"I'm listening, Tom," he said quietly. It was, surely, better to let Tom have his say than watch him spend his strength in fretting.

Tom spoke slowly, then, with long pauses between his sentences. "But how can I tell you?" he began. "Still, I must, since it concerns you closely." He sighed and coughed again. "I've been a poor steward of our inheritance from our father, Dickon. Our crops have failed when others' flourished. Our sheep died of strange sicknesses. Bad times came and came. And when the times *were* good, there was never enough to make up for the evil days. To make it short, Dickon, it's gone. All gone. Everything our father left us. The moneys. The lands. The sheep and cattle. Horses. All of it gone."

"Never mind, Tom," Dickon said. "You'll soon be well again and strong and we will prosper."

"No, Dickon. You don't understand the whole of it. I. . . ." Tom shook his head and began again on another sentence, leaving Dickon wondering what he had begun to say. "It's gone, lad. All gone. Seized to pay the debts the bad times laid upon me. The bailiffs hold off a little, but only because of this accursed illness."

"But—but, Tom." Dickon would not, at first, accept the full meaning of what he was hearing. In all his life he'd not given a thought to money. His father's lands had prospered. There'd always been plenty and to spare. How could Tom, in five short years, have brought them to ruin?

How could Dickon Fontayne continue his life at Cambridge if there were no funds to pay for the rest of his schooling?

He said, "Tom!" angrily, and looked at his brother and saw sadness and despair overlying the look of illness and checked his anger sharply. He could not let Tom see his feelings now.

But Tom had, already, seen. "You've good cause for anger," he said, "But it's no use. What's done is done."

He waited for some sign of reassurance from his younger brother and when Dickon held to his silence Tom went on, angry now in his turn though he was so weak he could not give his feelings force and the sound of his anger was no more than a whine. "It was not my fault, Dickon. It was the fault of the times. The times were bad, I tell you."

Dickon thought bad times came to all men, yet others somehow managed to keep their lands. But all he said was, "Let be, Tom. As you say, what's done is done."

He was silent again, remembering all the days in the past two years when Tom had been away from Chipping Norton—in France, in Scotland, even in Spain, following no man knew what pleasures of his own. If he had stayed at home, would the crops have prospered and the sheep stayed alive? But what good now, with Tom helpless and fretful, to chide him? Later, when he was well, they could have it out.

Tom moved restlessly in his bed and coughed again. Dickon lifted him higher on the pillows and was flooded with pity and aching affection at the weightlessness of the once burly body. He remembered Tom's gentleness and the kindness he'd always shown the small brother forever tagging at his heels. He remembered, too, the hours Tom had spent teaching him all the lore of the fields and forest and streams. Tom was not cut out to manage estates. He said, gently, "Don't fret, Tom. All will come right in the end. Somehow. Now ease your mind and rest."

Tom smiled a little, grateful for gentleness. The tenseness went out of his body, and he thrust back against the pillows and closed his eyes. Almost at once Dickon saw he had dropped asleep.

CHAPTER II

A Boon for Tom

Dickon sat and watched Tom's struggling breaths for long moments, deliberately keeping his mind blank. But he could not force his active thoughts to quiet. He could no longer still his mind.

Tom—his mind said—Tom did not expect to get well. So what if he were right? What if Tom were to die and leave Dickon alone and without money to make his way in a world he feared and did not understand?

He had no time to explore the thought, for Tom was awake as suddenly as he had fallen asleep and was going on as if there had been no interruption in his talk.

"You're a good lad, Dickon." His voice seemed to have gained all its old strength in the few minutes of sleep and Dickon felt encouragement drive away despair. "I knew you'd understand, given a little time. Now for the other thing."

"The other thing?" Dickon had forgotten Tom had spoken of a boon to be granted.

"Yes. An old comrade of mine walks in danger. You must warn him."

"Comrade?" Dickon asked and realized how little he knew of Tom's life or his friends.

"He lives in London," Tom went on as if Dickon had not spoken. "I don't know his lodgings but you can find them, I'm sure, for he's not a man unknown in these days. His name is Marlowe. Christopher Marlowe."

"Christopher Marlowe!" Dickon repeated the words as if Tom had named the angel Gabriel for friend. "You don't mean—you can't mean Kit Marlowe the playmaker? How could you be comrade to him?"

"Do you, too, know him, then?" Tom asked, surprised at the enthusiasm in Dickon's voice.

"Know him?" Dickon repeated. "Not as you mean it, Tom, for I've never seen him. But I know him by his writings. I had a friend at Cambridge, though he's been gone these two years to be a player, for that is what he wanted most and his father would deny him nothing. Robin Lang and I"—Dickon paused to laugh a little—"used to go about and about behind the backs of the masters and act Kit Marlowe's plays with others of like mind among our fellows. That was a merry time, I can tell you. I think," he added, sobering, "I do solemnly think Christopher Marlowe to be the greatest man in all England, maybe in all the world. For truth and the search for it is his very master. 'The mind must be still climbing after infinite and ever moving with the restless spheres.' Did you know he wrote those words, Tom? He wrote them in a play called *Tamburlaine* while he was still a scholar at Cambridge. And he wrote another thing in that same play. 'Nature that framed us in four elements, warring without our breast for regiment, doth teach us all to have aspiring minds.' 'Aspiring minds,' 'Climbing after infinite,' those are mighty words and the measure of a mighty mind. Is this your Marlowe, Tom?"

Tom, who had been only half listening, husbanding his strength, answered slowly, "Likely, for I've heard it said Kit Marlowe, my Kit Marlowe, was a fair poet. But I know little of that. When he and I were comrades, we were both upon the Queen's business."

Dickon, his mind still following the words of Marlowe the playmaker, and still held in thrall to them, asked absently, "The Queen's business?"

"Or Walsingham's, which is the same thing," Tom said and Dickon, plucked from his remembering by the name almost shouted, "Sir Francis Walsingham's business! Do you mean *spying*, Tom?"

"Spying, certainly," Tom said. "What else?"

"But—but that is a terrible thing. What right had Sir Francis Walsingham to use the greatest poet of the times as a spy? Suppose he were caught? Suppose he were *killed*? Suppose he never wrote another play? No! No, Tom. You must be wrong."

Tom said, wearily, "You speak as a child, Dickon. What does Francis Walsingham care for such things as

playmaking so long as the Queen's business is for-
warded? Remember, he is concerned with keeping
Elizabeth alive and on her throne and England safe
from plotters. Now will you stop interrupting me?"

"But, Tom. . . ."

"Hush, Dickon, and listen." The flush on Tom's
cheeks was worse and his voice had risen. Troubled as
he was over what he had heard, Dickon thought it best
to humor his brother. He nodded and Tom went on.

"You'd better know more of *my* Marlowe or you'll
likely not believe the rest of my tale. And you *must* believe it, Dickon. There's no one else to take my warning."

"Go on," Dickon said.

"Kit Marlowe and I, while we were still at Cambridge, went once together to France. We pretended to
be of the Roman faith, so that we could find out what
schemes against the Queen were hatching in that nest
of Jesuit plotters at Rheims. You know there's a school
at Rheims—a school for men seeking to destroy the
Protestant belief and the Queen and bring England
under the might of Spain."

He paused again and the pale ghost of remembered
mirth touched his eyes. "I went but the once, but Kit
was away from his studies much of the year. He bore
the brunt of the spying and it nearly lost him his master's degree."

"What?" Even the thought made Dickon angry.
"Why?"

"The chancellor took it into his addled head that

Kit was a renegade and a Papist. In those days, Dickon, there were many students who would just disappear from their colleges. Then, after a time, they would go to Rheims, for they were secretly of the Roman faith. They had been biding their time till they could show their true colors in safety."

Dickon nodded as Tom looked at him to see if he were following. Tom, he thought, sounded almost well and strong again.

"Now mind you, Dickon," Tom went on, "that was before Armada fight and not all that long since Catholic Mary was burning good Protestants for love of the Pope. Even today, there are those in this land who'd turn a blind eye and a deaf ear to any plot that would return the English Church to Rome."

His speech was getting faster and faster. Better remind him again, Dickon thought, of his student days, for that seemed to calm him. "So what happened to Christopher Marlowe and his master's degree?" he asked.

"Curse this fever for making me forget," Tom said. "Now where was I?"

"At the chancellor's refusal to give Marlowe his degree," Dickon said patiently.

"So. Well, Walsingham would have none of that, for he always looked after his own and Kit had given him good service. The Queen's own council ordered the degree bestowed on him, and there was nothing the chancellor could do about it. But you should have seen his face when he handed Kit the parchment."

He was quiet again. Dickon made no move to disturb the silence, glad of it for it gave him a moment to gather his thoughts into some semblance of order—or try to. But it was difficult for him to accept the things his brother had been saying so casually.

Marlowe, the great playmaker; Marlowe, who it was said feared nothing but false thinking; Marlowe, the man he'd most wish to copy in his own life; Marlowe, a *spy*! How dared anyone put so great a mind in jeopardy! Were there not plenty of lesser men Walsingham could have used for his purposes?

And Tom! Wasn't Tom saying he too had been Walsingham's cat's-paw? Was this—this Queen's business what had taken Tom to those far places? Was that what had brought them to ruin and Tom near to dying?

"Tom," he began, but the grip that had relaxed upon his wrist tightened and Tom said, "Another time, Dickon. Now you must pay close attention. I thought Kit had put such things behind him. For I, even I, had heard he was a playmaker now and London's darling. But I have come to believe he's still at the spying."

"Why?"

"I was, just recently, in France where I took so heavy a cold it brought me low and I had to lie at Dover and send for Peter to help me home. And while I burned and shivered in a hostel there, I heard things to frighten me."

Dickon said, "What things?"

"Men, I don't know how many or who they were, except one called another Frizer; they were talking in the room next to mine. They spoke of an ambush that would end in a killing. And they spoke the name of Kit Marlowe, spoke it with scorn and, it seemed to me, with bitter hate and fear. The devil of it was that, even then, this hell-brewed fever was upon me and there were times I went clean out of my wits and heard nothing, or only a jumble. So I could not learn the whole of this plot. But plot it was, of that I'm sure, and I fear for Kit for I'm sure those men mean to harm him. And he—he's afraid of neither God nor the devil, and he will take no care to himself unless he is well persuaded of clear danger. So, Dickon, since I'm laid low, you must haste to London and find him and give him my warning. It may be, coming from me, his comrade in spying, he will listen for he knows my ways and knows, too, I'm not easily made fearful."

The last words came haltingly and he stopped, gasping for the breath he'd spent recklessly in his need to send Dickon upon this errand.

Dickon sat in stillness. He was appalled by Tom's request. Go to London—great, unknown city and plague-ridden to boot—alone! His mind veered away from the very thought. How could he who had feared to make his way—though that, thank his stars, had proven easier than he had hoped—from Cambridge to Chipping Norton without blundering, find among London's myriad streets and lanes, swarming with thousands of people, the lodgings of one man? He couldn't do it. He knew he couldn't. He could not even think how to begin such a task.

One man in all those thousands! The very thought was ridiculous.

But the man was Christopher Marlowe and he was in danger. So, Dickon Fontayne, would-be scholar, must find him. He *must*! Somehow, he had to find the wit to discover the playmaker and save him. Somehow, he must make his way to London—alone. He half rose, thinking to begin the journey now, at once.

But what of Tom? He couldn't leave Tom, his well-loved brother, ill and alone except for an aging servant. He said, slowly, "I'll go, Tom. Of course, I'll go. Just as soon as you are better."

"No, Dickon. Don't you understand? There is no time. Go now!" He looked to the window and saw the westering sun showing already the colors of sunset and added, "Too late tonight. Tomorrow morning early, you must leave."

Dickon thought he could put Tom off a little with some of the practical thoughts that were hurling themselves at his own mind. For Marlowe or no Marlowe he could not leave Tom yet. He said, and tried to make his voice light and bantering as if he were speaking to a child, "But, Tom. I can't go off to London in the midst of the plague, without money to buy food and lodging. That will take a little time."

"I've thought it all out," Tom said, "while I waited for you to come from Cambridge." He fumbled in the bedclothes and brought out a small leather pouch.

"They say the plague's abating and, look, Dickon, here's our mother's ring of rubies. She gave it to me for you and I've kept it safe through all the troubled times. Take it to Shadrach of Malta in the lane beside the church in Chipping Norton. He'll give you good and honest value for it."

"Tom, Tom," Dickon said. "Don't you see I can't leave you, ill as you are? Surely a day or two while you mend will make no difference?"

Tom struggled to pull himself up in the bed and when Dickon laid a hand upon him, spoke wildly, his voice rising to a thin wail. "You will go, Dickon? For your love of me; for my concern for an old comrade; for—for the Queen of England since, I'm sure, Marlowe is still about her business and must not be stopped. Promise me, Dickon. Promise me!"

What could he do? He said, "I promise, Tom" and wondered what would happen tomorrow if Tom were no better and held him to his given word. He shook the thought from him. Surely, tomorrow Tom *would* be better. Already, having freed his mind of the things that had been troubling it, he had relaxed upon the pillows. Maybe all he needed was a long night of quiet sleep. Even the few minutes he had slept just now had seemed to give him new strength—at least for a while. Dickon got to his feet and started to tiptoe from the room.

A cough that ended quickly in a gasp turned him about. He saw Tom, sitting erect, his eyes wild and frightened. Two strides took Dickon back to the bed-

side. He put his arms about his brother, making sooth-
ing noises, trying to force the taut body back upon the
pillows. Tom gasped again, struggling to speak, to
breathe. "Dickon!" he said and the strain went out of
him and he lay, limp, in Dickon's arms.

Dickon eased him down upon the bed. "Tom," he
cried. "Tom, what is it? Shall I send Peter to fetch the
leech?"

There was no answer and he leaned over his brother
and could see no sign of breath. He stood watching the
motionless figure before he ran from the room shouting for Peter.

CHAPTER III

Highwayman

Peter came running and together he and Dickon stood beside the bed looking down at Tom's quiet figure, the face showing a little color from the dying sun. Dickon put out his hand and drew it back and looked at Peter. He said, knowing he was making a mock of the truth, "I'm sorry, Peter, I called you. He's only sleeping."

Peter leaned over and put his head upon his master's chest and listened. When he straightened again there were tears in the age-furrows of his face. "Oh, Master Dickon," he said, "no man can sleep without breathing."

"He cannot be dead! What will I do if Tom's not here? Go quickly, Peter. Get help. Fetch the leech."

Peter shook his head. He started to speak and stopped himself and went from the room to do Dickon's bidding, though he knew it to be useless.

Dickon pulled a chair close and sat beside the bed, watching Tom's quiet face, making his mind blank to hold back the fears that threatened him, until Peter came again with the physician. The doctor laid a hand upon Tom's heart and shook his head and went away leaving the old man and the boy to stare at one another, too dumb with grief to reach for comfort.

They walked next day behind the minister to the churchyard in Chipping Norton. Dickon stood as if he, too, were a clod, not hearing the solemn, beautiful service for the dead. When it was over the minister tried to say helping words; tried, too, to ask about Dickon's plans for the future and offer aid if it were needed. Dickon gave him, from long habit, courteous answers but they were without meaning. His mind was still frozen with shock and grief and he didn't know what he said. The minister, shaking his head a little, left thinking to try again later. Dickon and Peter went home in silence.

The next morning Peter came early to Dickon's room. "Master Dickon," he said, "if—if you would honor us, my wife and me—if you wouldn't mind our simple cottage, we would be proud to have you come and stay with us, until you can make your plans. We've enough and to spare put by from the good years and. . . ."

He saw Dickon was weeping and stopped in midsentence and cried out in distress, "Master Dickon!"

Dickon didn't try to stop the tears. He knew well enough he was too old for crying, but he felt the tears were, in some way he did not clearly understand, unblocking his mind. After a time, while Peter stood with his hand hard upon Dickon's shoulder, he swallowed a final sob and said, "Th—thank you, P—Peter. You know I would come to you gladly, but Tom"—he swallowed again on the word—"Tom laid a charge upon me and I promised to fulfill it. And now it is time to be about that business. It will take me to London and I'd better be on my way."

Peter said, "But, Master Dickon, you can't go to London. There's plague there and they say it's no safe place for any man, with people dying each day by the hundreds and hundreds, and the very streets little better than charnel houses."

"Still I must go," Dickon said.

He had, for a while, forgotten his promise to Tom, forgotten the danger to Christopher Marlowe. Remembering now, he was in a fever to get away, to leave behind him all the sad reminders of his boyhood and of Tom. If he took the plague and died of it, there would, at least, be no more decisions to make, no more fears and uncertainties about the future.

Peter seemed to sense further argument would be useless. He drooped his shoulders and said, "You will need money, Master Dickon."

Dickon hesitated. He felt a curious reluctance to speak of his mother's ring, even to Peter. It seemed, somehow, his last link with Tom and he wanted to hold the very knowledge of it close and secret in his heart.

"I have enough," he said. "Will you go now and make me a parcel of food, for I must get quickly to London and stop as little as possible on the way. With what food you can find for me I can eat as I go and so save a little time."

Peter started to argue and changed his mind and went away. Dickon collected a few essentials for travel, his razor and comb and the wedge of soap from the washhand stand. He folded them inside his cloak, leaving it open for what food Peter would bring.

When the old man returned with the packet, he was carrying as well a bag that held three golden balls.

"Remember the time I told you of when my wife and I gave shelter to a juggler taken ill upon the road?" he asked.

Dickon wrinkled his forehead, remembering, before he nodded, a half-forgotten winter when Peter had showed him the juggler's balls left as recompense for a month of shelter and care. He remembered Peter's skill with them and the hours he'd spent in Peter's cottage learning, for his own amusement, to juggle the smooth and shining globes.

"Take them with you, Master Dickon," Peter said. "There are always fools and gulls in the towns who will throw away their pennies—even their shillings—for a juggling show. If you need money, the balls will bring it to you."

"But—but they are yours, Peter. I remember how proud you were of them and how skillful in their use. I cannot take them from you. Besides, I doubt I could remember what to do with them."

Peter shoved the bag into his hand. "Take them, Master Dickon," he ordered. He held out his hands, twisted and swollen with rheumatism. "The balls are no more use to me now. And you will not have forgotten your skill with them, nor with the other tricks I taught you those many years ago. The hand does not easily forget its cunning and a few minutes of practice with those as you go along your way will bring you quickly up to snuff with them."

Dickon took the bag and tied it at his waist. He could find no words to thank Peter, but he gripped the old man's shoulder hard before he tied up his pack and went from the room and from the house where he had been born.

He made little progress that day. He wasted the whole morning and part of the afternoon trying to find Shadrach of Malta. The small house huddled in the lane behind the church was shut and bolted when he came to it. He waited a time, kicking restlessly at the stones under his feet, hoping the owner would return quickly. Then he set out along the stream that meandered through the village, and crossed the bridge at its end and knocked at all the doors of the thatched-roof, stone cottages wandering up the slope beyond. No one knew anything of Shadrach or, it seemed to Dickon, wanted to. In one of the houses a woman, leaning from a window to shake out her bedding, berated him for disturbing her at her work with his questions. An old, bent man leaned on a spade to rest from his work of turning the ground beneath an early-blooming rose and talked on and on about Armada fight and the wound he'd had there and the glory of battling cheek by jowl with the great Captain Drake himself, for the saving of Queen Elizabeth and confusion to the might of Spain.

By the time Dickon could get away from him and ask at the last house on the hillside, the noonstead was long past and he was none the wiser about Shadrach's whereabouts. He went back along the way he had come, back once more to the house in Church Lane, but it was still tight shut.

What should he do? He would not get far this day in any case. Likely he'd not get far on any day without the money the rubies would bring. Even with the money he'd be long, for there would likely not be enough for a horse and it would take him ten days at the least, he reckoned, to walk the miles to London.

He knew he should go back to Peter and start over on the morrow. But he hated the thought of returning to the house that was no longer home. Besides, remembering Tom's urgency, his mind told him he must get on, and must let nothing delay him. Tom would have known what to do.

Tom! Tom was dead. Tom would never again counsel him what to do about this or that. Now he must learn to decide for himself whether to go this way or that way, to make this decision or that one. Well then, he'd go on and make as much distance as he could before night found him. With discouragement walking close upon his heels, he began the long journey to London. If only he had a horse!

When the falling night caught him less than ten

miles from home—or what had been home—he felt he would never reach his goal. He touched the wash-leather pouch that held the ruby ring. What good was it to him? If he went to the inn in the next village, of-fered the ring as payment for his lodging, the inn-keeper would surely suspect him of thievery and call the constable and that would be the end of his journey. For who was there to stand surety for his tale of having the rubies from his mother? Not even Peter knew about it.

Likely he'd have to sleep on the bare ground. Unless he could find a barn or sheepcote where he could sneak in unseen. He wished with all his might he had the courage to go up to the first house he found and ask for shelter. But fear of being turned away and, likely, cursed to boot, made him shudder from the thought. Knowledge of such things were not learned at Cambridge.

He'd better start his seeking, for the nights were chilly. Already he was shivering in his thin clothes. He stopped in the path across the fields he'd been travel-ing and looked about him and saw, a little distance off, a flickering light—a rushlight probably, though what difference that made he didn't know. It had sprung alive even as he watched in the gathering twilight, and he went toward it. There was, indeed, a cow byre, not too near the farm cottage where the light showed. He crept toward it, almost holding his breath lest he rouse a watchdog to bay a warning of his presence. But ei-ther there was no dog or it was lolling inside the cottage, warm by the fire. Thinking of that good heat, he shivered even more violently. He took a deep breath and pushed open the door of the byre and went into its shelter.

It smelled of old fodder and the breath of the cow that moved restlessly at his coming. Holding the door ajar, he inspected the little hut by the last of the evening light and saw the pile of hay in a corner a little apart from the animal's stall. Before he closed the door, he took careful bearings; then, in the blackness, he felt his way along the walls until his searching foot found the hay pile. He fell upon it, too tired to eat any of the food in the parcel Peter had made him.

The soft lowing of the cow awoke him the next morning. Sunshine was creeping through space between the hut's siding. He jumped up, wondering whether he was already too late to avoid discovery. Not even taking time to brush the sticky hay wisps from his clothes, he cracked the door and squeezed through and just managed to get himself out of sight in a little copse of oaks before he heard the farmer, grumbling to himself about cows that had to be milked at break of day. When, from his shelter, he saw the man pause at the door, still cracked as he had left it, and scratch his head, Dickon turned and ran for the path before the outlines of his body in the hay pile should betray his use of the byre as a retiring room.

This was the pattern of his traveling for three more endless, lonely days, though there was not always a convenient shelter to be found. He longed for some companionship, someone, even some creature to talk to, but he was afraid of being stopped and delayed further if he veered from the byways he was choosing. He made slow progress, for midway through the second day his feet, unaccustomed to day-long walking over rough land, began to ache and he was forced to stop more and more often to rest their burning. Though he ate sparingly of the bread and cheese and cold beef Peter had found for him, he knew the food would not last much longer. Toward the evening of his fourth day upon the road, it began to rain: a fine, cold, drizzle of damp that seeped into his very bones. He looked about him, hoping to find a farm or even a single house where he might, if despair would only lend him courage, force himself to beg a night's lodging. But the land stretched on all sides empty of human habitation.

Were it not for the rain, he would lie down here in the middle of the vague and wandering path he was following over the downs and give in to the despair that filled him. How could he ever have thought he could make his way to London alone? He had avoided the roads with their milestone markers, fashioned, so he'd learned, after the Roman custom. He didn't know how far he had yet to go and he felt he would never reach London and discharge Tom's last request.

A bird call shook him out of his thoughts. He looked toward the sound and saw a flash of brilliant black and white against the rain-dulled sky. He watched the bird, a cuckoo he thought, as it winged toward the horizon and lost it in the foliage of a tree he had not, in his preoccupation with himself, noticed before. A tree would provide at least a small shelter from the rain. He plodded toward it and found a great copper beech. It must be older than time, for it had grown to an enormous height. Furthermore, its lowest branches swept the ground and made a snug shelter, dry and almost warm. He crawled in among the boughs and unwrapped his cloak from about the bundle of his belongings and shrouded himself in it. He ate a shriveled winter apple that had been near the bottom of the parcel of food and lay upon the ground to sleep.

When he awoke next morning the May sunrise was filling the world with color. Far ahead he could make out the spires and squat towers of a town. For the first time since Tom had died his heart lifted a little. Oxford. It must be. There was no other place nearby larger than a village. Oxford was a town of some size and where there was a town there would be people and where there were people there would be a gathering of fools and gulls to spend their pennies for entertainment. He had practiced his old tricks once while he was traveling and had found Peter had been right about the hand and its cunning. And here, at last, was hope of getting at least a little of the money he needed so badly.

But first he must find a stream. He stood beside the tree and turned slowly about. From the rise he could see a fair distance across the grassy downs, and it was no more than a minute before his eyes caught a glimmer of gold that was a stream reflecting the sunrise glow and, beyond it, a curving ribbon of bare earth that must be the high road to Oxford.

He began to walk cautiously toward the stream, testing the soreness of his feet. To his relief he found them less painful than they had been. He walked faster and faster until, by the time he came to the rivulet at the foot of the hill, he was almost running. He spread his cloak upon the ground and took out the razor and comb and soap. He knelt beside a small, clear pool in the stream and grimaced at his face mirrored in it. He did look a very villain. Carefully, he scraped off the stubble of beard and washed away the grime he had picked up on the road. When he had combed the tangles out of his dark curls that capped his head and brushed at his clothes with a bit of willow branch, he felt and looked a different person. As he rewrapped his bundle, hope quickened in him and with it a fresh urgency about the task Tom had set him. He must get to Marlowe.

He stepped quickly through the screen of willows that hid the roadway from him and said, aloud, to encourage himself, "Well, Dickon Fontayne, you've come so far at least. And alone, without help or even advice. If you walk with Luck, you may get to London. Please heaven it will be in time."

And suddenly he felt an altogether new and disproportionate pride in himself as if he had accomplished some great feat of daring. "Oxford," he shouted to the fresh day, "I'm coming!" and started down the road.

"HALT!"

The command came from just ahead of him and he obeyed it out of astonishment. It was followed by the appearance from among the fringe of roadside bushes of a figure in what had once been the clothes of a courtier, though they were crusted now with dirt and were ragged. The figure wore a mask and a broad-brimmed hat, much too large, that flopped about the face, leaving it in deep shadow. The highwayman, for such Dickon took the apparition to be, held an enormous pistol and held it in both hands, trying, without success, to still its wobbling.

The effect was so comical that, in spite of the gun pointed at him, Dickon burst out laughing. Surely an inexperienced highwayman, this!

The laugh was short-lived. A gun was a gun and if the person who held it were unaccustomed and fearful, anything could happen. Still, guns were things he was accustomed to and he thought he could throw himself out of the way before this one could be cocked which, he could see, it was not. Very slowly, he started walking toward the gun-holder and saw the pistol bob up and down like a willow wand in the hands of a water diviner. The highwayman began to back away before him and Dickon laughed again, shortly.

"I'm your first victim, I'll be bound," he said conversationally, "and likely your last unless you can keep your hand—and one hand at that—steady on your weapon. You'll need the other to relieve me of my purse, you know, or would need it if I had a purse which I haven't."

"Keep away from me! Do you not come one step closer or—or I'll shoot!" The voice that had been low-pitched and growly upon the single word, "Halt," was suddenly high and shrill.

Dickon took the remaining distance between them in one jump. He jabbed at the pistol and it flew to one side as the hands that held it went limp with terror. Dickon snatched away the floppy hat and stood back to stare at the mass of red-gold hair that fell about the would-be highwayman's shoulders.

"So!" he said. "It's as I guessed. A girl! Whatever made you think you could force a man to stand still while you robbed him?"

The girl put her hands over her face and Dickon thought she was crying. Just like a girl. What did you do with a crying woman? All his shyness plus embarrassment came back upon him and made him angry. He reached out and snatched the hands away and wondered if a good hard slap would dry the tears.

But the girl was not crying. She looked, indeed, as angry as he. "The Devil take you!" she said. "Now you've spoiled it. You might have let me p—practice on you."

"Practice on me!" Dickon felt as if he had been in some manner insulted. Practice on him indeed!

"Yes, practice. I meant you no harm. The pistol is not even loaded. And it's plain to see you're no rich merchant. But how can I learn to rob a rich man if I have had no chance to practice being a—a highwayman?"

Dickon said, "Who in the name of Lucifer are you, and what are you doing crying *halt* to lonely gentlemen even if you would only practice on them?"

The girl ignored the question. She spoke arrogantly, ordering him as if she were Queen Elizabeth herself, "I'm hungry. Give me food."

Dickon stared at her, fury at her high-handed manner turning his face crimson. Who did she think she was demanding to be fed as if he were her lackey? He had little enough without sharing it with a—a strumpet who'd just tried to rob him.

"Have you lost your wits?" he asked. "Why should I give you food? I've barely enough for myself. Why should I share what I have with a road robber?"

The girl's brief spate of anger left her and she looked forlorn and miserable. "I—I'm so hungry," she said in a thin, little-girl's wail.

Dickon, against his will, pitied her. His mind swung between lingering outrage at her attempted assault upon his limited rations and a growing feeling that he wanted, in some way, to help her. Compassion won the struggle and he said, a little sullen and more than a little reluctant still, "Oh, very well. I do have a little food. Not much. Come along here to the verge of the road and we'll eat it. I've had no breakfast myself. But you're to take only a little, mind."

She followed him, and when he had opened the food

parcel would have snatched all it contained had he not stopped her. "Not so fast, my lady," he said. "There's no more and the good Lord only knows how long this little must last us."

He heard the last word in amazement. What was he doing, offering to share what bit of food was left with this waif of the road! He squinted sidewise at her, hoping she had not heard him or had not realized the implication of that *us*. He let out his breath in relief for her whole attention seemed to be upon the bread and cheese he had doled out to her.

His relief didn't last long. No sooner had the food disappeared and he had shaken his head at the unspoken request for more than she said, "Perhaps you're right. We'd better keep what we have until I can plan to get us more."

"Us?" he said, pretending to be unaware of having yoked the girl to his future plans. "The food is mine, not yours. Who said anything about us?"

"You did," she answered promptly—and pertly. The small amount of food seemed to have restored her courage. She sounded cock-sure again, too cock-sure for his comfort. "Besides," she added, "you need me as much as I need you or I don't know an innocent when I see one."

"I? Need *you*? You *are* witless. I've work to do, girl, and you'd be nothing but a hindrance to the doing of it."

"So? And where are you going so early in the morning?"

"To London, if it's any concern of yours."

She paid no heed to his increasing irritation. "And have you a permit to travel the roads or the price of a night's lodgings in silver in your purse?"

"That I have not. But what matter? What English gentleman—and that I am, you know—needs a permit to travel in his own country?"

She looked him up and down. "I'll vow you don't have the look of gentle birth about you. Besides, the Queen's law reads you must have a permit or money in your purse to prove you're no vagabond nor yet one of the scurvy crew who pretends to be a soldier returned from the wars and shows great, ugly, festering wounds to loosen the purse strings of the unwary rich and great. Not that the wounds are, for the most part, anything but powder and paint, but who's to look too close?"

Dickon stared at her. He felt as if a blow to his stomach had driven the breath out of his body. His mind, numbed by the shock of her statements, tried to wrestle with this new problem and could not. Why had he not, in his quiet sanctuary at Cambridge, paid more attention to the ways of the world outside?

"But!" The girl's voice was buzzing in his ear, interrupting his pity for himself. She was waving a piece of paper under his nose. He brushed it away irritably but in the next instant it was back again. "See what I have?" she jeered. "A permit for three people to go where they will. And it has still a month to run. Now do you see that you need me as much as I need you?

With this no busybody of a constable can make trouble for you. Or for me, in your company."

His head felt thick still. Things were happening too rapidly for him. "But—but," he said, "I—I don't even know your name or how you came to be waving a pistol at me in the middle of the high road to Oxford. And how will I ever get to London with a girl as a tag?"

"Faugh!" she said. "How will you get there without me? You must be as stupid as you look. My name, if it matters so much to you, is Cicely and if you'll stop your dithering I'll tell you how I came here—through no fault of my own, I can promise. But we'd best get a little away from the road, for it won't be long," she looked at the sun, now well above the horizon, "before we'll have company in plenty."

CHAPTER IV

Lost Child

Dickon followed the girl back through the screen of willows to a stretch of grass already dried of its night's dew. It would be a hot day and he wished he were alone so he could strip off his clothes and bathe in the little pool he'd used earlier.

Cicely settled herself comfortably on the grass and looked at him. He stood where he was, staring down at her, trying to bring some order to his floundering mind. There should, if all his studying meant anything, be some small thread of logic in what was happening, but he could not find it.

"Well," she said impatiently, "will you sit down and hear my story or will you not? I can scarcely tell it with my neck stretched like a camelbird to see you. Time won't stand still for your mooning, and London is still a week away—if we're lucky."

He shook his head a little and dropped down beside her. "Go on," he said, "I'm listening." He sounded, even to himself, angry. Well, why shouldn't he be? It was enough to make a very saint angry, having this complication come when he'd just begun to think he could make his own way. But whatever could he do with a girl at his heels? It would have been hard enough without her. Why didn't he get up and leave her now?

He knew why, of course. It was that bit of paper she held. Why hadn't he known he would need a permit to travel? Or silver in his purse? That was what came of losing himself in studies and giving no thought to what went on in the world outside his university.

She had the right of it. He needed her—or her permit—as much or more than she needed him. He frowned, thinking how quick each town and village was to pass paupers on to the next one, once their own workhouses were full. It was hard to be poor.

"You're not listening," she said and he jerked his mind back.

"I am, too." He hoped she wouldn't try to make him prove it.

She gave him a look that seemed to say he was a fool if he thought he could dupe her so.

"I don't know who I am," she began and sounded bored. He thought she must have said this before and he hadn't heard it.

"Don't *know*—don't know who you *are*?" He wondered if somehow in the last three days, his ears had been bewitched. How could anybody not know who they were?

"Be quiet and listen," she said. "I—do—not—know —who—I—am. Only what I've been these many years past. My mother and my father—for so they claimed to be—called themselves 'knights of the road.' In truth they were vagabonds wandering where their fancy took them, getting their living by—well by means *you'd* not approve of, to judge by the smug look of you. But let me tell you, what's-your-name. . . ."

"Dickon Fontayne."

"Then let me tell you, Dickon Fontayne, there are many folk abroad in this land who have not your luck."

My luck, Dickon thought, bitterly. Little does she know of my luck. He was beginning to loathe this girl.

"But," she went on, not noticing the look he gave her, "I am not their child. I know it. Know it in my bones and my flesh. I can even remember—a long, long ago and faintly. But it's a true memory for all that—a memory of merry folk and a great, friendly house with gardens and orchards, and hands apt to gentleness."

Rubbishy nonsense, Dickon thought. Just like a girl with no logic in her to imagine an elegant past for herself because she didn't like her own way of life. Truth she lacked, this Cicely. Any real notion of truth at least. He started to put the thought into words and saw her eyes, looking past him into sadness, and felt pity for her again and held his tongue. Why destroy her dreams? They did him no harm.

"Well," he said when she looked as if she'd not find

her way back to reality without prompting. "Do they beat you, then, this un-father-and-mother?"

"Beat me?" She seemed still half in some secret place of her mind which she was loathe to leave. She gave herself a little shake and said again, "Beat me? Oh yes. I've had beatings enough—and starvings and cursings —when I did not pick enough pockets of rich gentlemen on the road to their liking."

"You—you don't mean that. You couldn't. Picking pockets indeed."

"You'd not understand, of course," she said. "Though you may before we come at last to London. You'd not know of the villainous folk who steal young children—or buy them sometimes—and teach them to be thieves and pickpockets—or worse—so their so-called parents can live in lazy comfort and safety."

Dickon started to protest again but she would not hear him. "But no matter," she went on, "the beatings and the cursings and the rest of it—they're over now."

Dickon shook his head. These things she was saying —surely they, too, must be true only in her imagination. But even as he tried to push the horrors of such a life from him, some part of his mind acknowledged this kind of thing must be real, for no one would build dreams around such beastliness.

"Over?" he said, picking up the end of her sentence. "Did you run away then?" Poor thing. In the end she'd not been able to go on in such lawless ways and had tried to free herself.

"Fool!" she said. "Do you think they'd *let* me run

away? Or that I'd have a place to run *to*? Or would
dare, of my own will, to risk my very life away from
such protection as they gave me? No. They took the
plague, first one, then the other, and died of it three
days ago."

"The plague!" Dickon began to pull away from her.
It was one thing to think of the plague off in London
and quite another to think he sat close beside its conta-
gion. How dared she?

"Oh, you've no cause to fear me," she said and
seemed to scorn him for his withdrawal. "I took the
sickness myself, but it touched me lightly, as it does
now and again, and left me safe. You'll not take the
plague from me. For everyone knows, once recovered
from it, a person is clean forever. But they died of it.
And a good riddance."

"What did you do, then?" Dickon asked. He was,
now, interested beyond his expectation in her story.

"What could I do? Hateful as they were to me, they
kept their watch over me. Once they'd taught me all
the arts of thievery, I was valuable to them, you see.
For he who called himself my father was always in
need of money for his gaming. Oh yes," she answered
the question in Dickon's eyes, "there's plenty of gaming on the road, as there is everywhere else in the
whole world I reckon. I tried to find some other pro-
tector to attach myself to—a family of jugglers or
strolling players—but times are hard for the vagabond
people, with the plague closing many of the towns and
the soldiers home from the wars and the Queen always

in need of money. So, in the end, I thought to put my skills to my own use. I took the pistol and these men's clothes and set out for a high lawyer—highwayman to you. I thought it would be easy to rob on the road for the rich are always more afraid for their lives than for their purses. And then you came along and spoiled it. No," she corrected herself, "to be honest about it, you came along and showed me I'd not the fortitude for a high lawyer."

"But," Dickon said, "I don't understand. Why. . . ."

"Are you witless?" She spat the interruption at him, her eyes full of anger. "Don't you know the plight of a girl, alone with the rabble that haunts the road? It's every man for himself and the devil take the hindmost and any woman without protection is fair game. I won't have it, I tell you. I'm no common trull and I'll not be made one. I was born of gentle folk, no matter that you don't believe it. And I'll not be the light o' love of such scourings, nor come on some county to spend the rest of my days in the workhouse. I can find work for myself. And I will if I can only get to London. In that plague-ridden city a plague-safe worker will be welcome, I can tell you. You—you *will* take me with you?"

The anger had gone and the bluster and left her woebegone. For the first time there were tears in her eyes and, as if for shame at them, she bent her head to her knees and covered it with her arms.

Dickon got up and walked a little away from the bowed figure. He was filled with horror at her story—

at the things said and, even more, at the things left un-
said that hinted at a degradation beyond his imagining. Compassion for her grew as he watched her
struggle to control the sobs that were shaking her. She
had a pitiful look in the scarecrow clothes which were
all the protection she had now. He guessed she was unused to tears and resented them. She didn't, to his
mind, have the look of a gentlewoman, with her rough
hands and sun-toughened skin, but she had the pride.
And now she had given him another chance to leave
her behind.

He stood, not looking at her, trying to think what
was best to do. He would, he guessed, have trouble
enough taking care of himself among the kinds of people she had suggested walked the roads. And, in spite
of the ridiculous tatters she wore, she'd give her sex
away every time she opened her mouth. But he—he
must get on with his warning to Marlowe. That feeling of urgency that had sent him ahead without waiting for Shadrach of Malta was with him now, pressing
him to hurry.

He *must* get to Marlowe in time. For Christopher
Marlowe had become in his mind more than a single
human being whose life was in danger, more than the
darling of the London crowds. This man had achieved
greatness—greatness for himself, greatness for England, greatness in a way for all men, with his fearless
mind which could not only seek truth and find it, but,
miraculously it seemed to Dickon, put that truth into
soaring, searing words that could charge other minds

to "climb after infinite." Marlowe was more than a mere human being. He was a symbol of England and England's greatness, and he must be saved.

Then, what of Cicely? For she would surely delay him. More, she was, by her own admission, a thief. Who could say when she would steal again and be caught and he, being her companion, be tarred with the stick of her lawlessness? All this he must now weigh against the balance of the travel permit she carried. And against something in the girl herself that tugged at his heart and urged him not to abandon her.

What would Tom say? Tom would say leave her. Forget the permit. Trust in his stars until he came to some place where he could exchange the rubies for the money that would be his safe passport the rest of the way. Till then, Tom would say, keep off the roads, keep away from towns, and forget the empty belly.

Well, that was it. He'd not take her with him. He put his hand on her shoulder thinking to show her he was not without concern for her though he must cast loose from her. He felt her body go rigidly still as if she had drawn in upon herself like a frightened rabbit.

He heard himself say, "Yes, Cicely, I'll take you."

CHAPTER V

Knights of the Road

He was appalled at the words. What had come over him that his thinking had somersaulted between a thought and a word? It was not so the hours of studying logic and philosophy had taught him to do. Angry with his own feckless mind, he transferred the anger to her and spoke roughly.

"But, I'll take you only if you do exactly as I say. Do you understand?"

She nodded her still-bowed head, but she did not raise it to show him her eyes. Her body lost its rigidity and had a collapsed look about it as if it had been a rag baby cast aside by a petulant child. He wanted to shake her, to grab her hair and pull her head up and make her look at him. He shut his fingers into fists against the urge and went on. "You are not to steal. No matter if we starve. No matter what happens. YOU ARE NOT TO STEAL. Not so much as a farthing."

She did look at him then.

"Not steal!" she said as if he had warned her not to breathe. "But how do you live on the road if you don't steal? Do you think bread grows on the trees and the birds will bring you meat? If you're hungry and there is no money to buy food, you take what you need from the rich people. What's wrong with that, I ask you?"

"Wrong with it?" Dickon shouted at her in his frustration. "Wrong with it? It's against the law, for one thing. And it's—it's not right. Did you never hear the commandment, 'Thou shalt not steal'?"

"Pooh," Cicely said. "If you're hungry you find a way to eat. If. . . ."

He let her get no further. "Cicely," he said and his voice, though it was quiet enough, had something in it that warned her against further agument. "Cicely-of-the-road, if you want my company, my—my protection, you will mark well what I say. *You are not to steal.* What's more, you are not to open your mouth when there's anyone in earshot. Not for one single word. If you fail, just once, to remember these two cautions, I will—I most solemnly swear it—I will leave you and not think twice about it."

"But, Dickon. . . ."

"There are no buts. You'll promise me and you'll not forget that promise, if you don't want to be left to get on as best you may. And I'll not take the time to warn you again either."

She said, softly and as solemnly as if she had been in church on Good Friday, "I won't forget. I do promise." Then, with a bewildering change of mood, she got up and stood beside him and shook herself. She grinned at him, an impish grin that seemed to taunt him. "But," she went on, "I'd just like to know how you plan to feed us when the victuals in your sack are gone, if *I* don't get the necessary?"

Dickon was irritated afresh with her. What did she think he was? A foolish bumpkin unable to find food? And care for her since she'd forced herself upon him. He'd show her. Show her, not tell her.

"You'll see," he said and had the satisfaction of seeing a look of uncertainty come into her face. "And don't forget what I've said. I'll have no thievery and no talking when others are about."

He turned away from her and picked up his bundle and started on, not looking to see—or caring—whether she followed him.

He parted the willows and drew in his breath as he saw the road. Where there had been emptiness and stillness there were noise and color and movement. The road, the whole world it seemed to him, had come alive with people. Why, all England must be on its way to Oxford!

Beggars whined their pleas for pennies, showing, some of them, the filthy, running sores Cicely had spoken of. The ugly spots looked so real he could not believe they were counterfeit. Peddlers and tinkers with their leather-strapped canvas bags on their backs hurried along, followed by mangy dogs. A huge brute of a man, leading a bear on a chain, passed so close Dickon could have reached through his willow-cover and touched the creature. There, was a man with a lute over his shoulder, and there, a group walked beside a cart piled with the gear of a band of strolling players. They reminded Dickon of Robin Lang and he was, for a moment, almost overcome with an ache to see his old friend. But at once his mind was diverted from such thoughts by the sight of a slim, young man on a horse pushing his way through the crowd with cries of "Make way there. Out of my way, villains," and the like. He was dressed in the very top of fashion with a great stiff ruff and enormous puffed sleeves. His doublet was so short it seemed to disappear at the saddle and his hose were elaborately embroidered with dozens of small pink and yellow roses. He held a pouncet box between finger and thumb, and Dickon could smell the oversweet reek of its perfume even where he stood. He thought the fop had little need to keep putting the box to his nose, not here where the good air washed over the evil smells.

One of the many children began to wail and a woman cuffed it quiet. Fascinated, Dickon couldn't take his staring eyes from the tatterdemalion lot. Most of the wanderers were dressed in clothes that were ragged or patched though each, it seemed, boasted a pair of shoes, hob-nailed or soundly pegged. He wondered if his own shoes, far less sound, would last the way to London.

This was a whole new world—a world he had not known or at least had not thought of, at Cambridge. He had paid scant attention to his companions of the road on his infrequent journeys between Cambridge and Chipping Norton. If those roads had been as teeming as this he had taken no note of it. Perhaps there was less traffic. And, of course, he had been well-mounted and more concerned with his horse than with the footpath way and the people on it. And of course he'd had Peter with him then. Now—now he was, or was about to become, a very part of this motley crowd and his mind swung between eagerness to join them and a distaste at the very thought. He snapped his fingers at himself. He'd better forget the distaste for there was no help for it. And he'd better be on his way. He had, already, wasted too much time.

He started to step out and join the throng, but he felt a hand on his arm, gripping hard to detain him. He had forgotten Cicely.

"Wait," she said quietly. "You'd better know something of them, for many could be dangerous to you." She waved her hand toward the road. "Besides since you—you're so nice in your judgment of folk, it would be well if you learn which to avoid for the sake of your gentlemanship's tender conscience."

He stepped a little away from her, feeling foolish and resenting it that she had made him feel so. She was right, though. It would be well to learn which of the road people were best avoided. But he hated to seem a complete fool before her.

"Tell me, then, but quickly," he said grudgingly.

"You should know, first, there are both evil men and poor unfortunates who walk the roads. Some have lost

their lands, being no doubt feckless, and must beg
their bread. Some have been dispossessed by the sheep
men. Others, jugglers, traveling troupes of players, are
honest enough, offering their shows in exchange for
money. But there are some, many of them, who are
dangerous."

"How do you know the one from the other, the
good, poor folk from the rascals?"

"You know," she said. "You know by the signs. You
learn them early or you don't survive. Look. Do you
see that short, fat, jolly-looking man with a rope hung
from his waist?"

Dickon nodded.

"He's a prigger of prancers, in spite of his smooth,
smiling face."

"A *what?*"

She looked her disgust at his ignorance and answered him loftily. "A horse stealer. And just beyond
there's a courber or angler." She waited for his question and when it didn't come, for Dickon was determined she'd not make him seem a fool again, she went
on with her explanation anyway. "He's a snatcher. He
snatches things away from houses—through a window
—or clothes hung on the line to dry. He's quick as a
lightning bolt, takes his spoils and goes, and no one
the wiser."

"But how?" Dickon was finding a kind of fascination
in this talk and had forgotten his determination not to
ask questions. His interest flattered her and she began
to speak again more patiently.

"He carries a jointed rod with a hook at its end. You can just see the tip beneath that one's cloak. He's a careless lout to let it show. You know, I can do that," she sounded proud, "or could, if I'd not left my rod behind."

She waited for some comment and when none came, she said, "Oh look! There's a nip."

"A—nip?"

"A cutpurse. See his knife? It's extra sharp as he is extra clever. He can snip away a purse and the owner not feel a thing or guess he's been robbed. And there, walking a distance from him, head high in disdain, is a foist. You can tell them easily for they are always at pains to look the gentleman, though they're nothing but pickpockets. You've little cause to fear from such as these, for its plain to see you've nothing in your pockets worth the stealing. But beware the uprightmen."

She stopped and shivered and he said, "Yes? Yes? Who are the uprightmen?"

"They are, in truth, the worst of the lot. They're the strongest of the vagabonds and they force the weaker to pay them tribute. I hate them."

The crowd had begun to thin somewhat and she was silent, watching it. Dickon moved restlessly. "Come," he said after a moment, "we'd best be going."

"Not yet. Soon the road will be empty again, or nearly so. I've seen a face or two I know in that crowd. Let them get well ahead. No use asking for trouble since you're so mighty afraid of traveling with a girl."

Dickon was grateful for her caution, even though it was tinged with scorn. But he wished she would not be eternally belittling him. He said, gruffly, "Very well," and added, as once more his curiosity got the better of his pique, "but why are they all together like this? Do they always move in batches?"

"No, ninny. The day is just starting. These people sleep where night finds them, and now they are hurrying to get to the town for, likely, it's market day— when people are careless and there's money to be found easily. This—batch as you call it, as if they were bread a-baking, slept nearby. It will take others longer to come up to this place."

"Then we'd better hurry, too," Dickon said as the stream on the road dwindled to a trickle.

"Why?"

"To go to the market."

"Do you, then, have a thing to sell?"

"Maybe. You'll see." He was determined not to tell her of his skill with the balls and japes. Let her find out for herself. Besides, it could just be he'd find another Shadrach of Malta to give him money for his jewel, and that would confound her right enough. He started to part the bushes and go out upon the road but, once more, she stopped him. This time she jerked him down so hard he almost sat on her. ·

"By the saints, what is it now?" he asked.

"Hush!" She made sure he obeyed her warning by putting her hand over his mouth. After a minute or

two she took it away and said, "Whew!" before she explained.

"There were two men, just passing. Jackdaw and
Sparrow they call themselves and I'd as leave not see
them again."

"Why?"

"Because." She began to answer and stopped, and
thought as if she were a little puzzled in her own mind
how to state her reasons clearly. "There are really two
becauses, I think," she went on. "There's a because for
each man. The Jackdaw because is easy. He traveled
with us once—a time ago—and he might know me
again, though I doubt it, in these clothes. He was more
than a little stupid, as I remember him, but he seemed
kindly. And he was well enough liked by the other
road people. But seeing him now with Sparrow. . . ."
Her voice trailed off as she stared toward the road.

Dickon, impatient of her silence, asked, "Why does
seeing him with the other trouble you?"

"I'm not just sure," she said slowly, "for they may
have met by chance and will soon separate again. It's
not always fair to judge a person by the company he's
keeping. But that Sparrow! He's not been long upon
the road but already terrible things are spoken of him.
Or so I heard him that called himself my father say. I
never cared enough to ask what things, though now I
wish I had. But this I do know. He's mean and boasts
himself a masterless man. And that lot is not above
anything so long as it will bring a shilling or get them

their own way. Yet, I do not understand why the two travel together. I'd take my oath on it, Jackdaw's a gentle creature by nature."

Dickon looked through the screen of trees and saw two backs disappearing down the road. A tall, brawny back and a slight, stringy back. He thought there was little to fear from the big one, for his walk was shambling and awkward and spoke of small skill in the big body. He'd wrestled with many such in the days when Peter was teaching him how to protect himself, and he knew they generally lacked real strength. He was not so sure about the smaller man, for he seemed better put together. But, Dickon thought, he wasn't afraid of that one either. He knew a trick or two of fighting he'd learned from Peter. He'd say nothing of this to Cicely. She'd only scoff at him again. Thought she knew everything, that girl did.

"They're gone now," he said, "and I'll wait no longer. You may come with me or stay, as you like. I've wasted too much time already."

He started up the road and, hard upon his heels, heard the clop of her following footsteps. Even she, he thought, wryly, had stouter shoes than he. But, thank the stars that governed all men's fortunes, his feet no longer hurt.

CHAPTER VI

Fools and Gulls

They came into Oxford half an hour later over the bridge guarded by the graceful tower of Magdalen College and caught their breaths at the sweep of the High Street. They gaped at the squat, stepped mass of St. George's Tower with the castle and chapel beneath it, but they walked in silence. Cicely was, for the time at least, mindful of the warning not to speak, and Dickon's eyes and mind were busy examining the close, dark lanes that ran away from the street. The façades of the colleges reminded him a little of his own university, though to him, they were nowhere near so beautiful. But they brought such a flood of recollections, he forgot where he was and would have stumbled over a stone and fallen flat in the roadway if Cicely had not put out a hand to stop him.

"Ninny-hammer!" she muttered under her breath. "Look where you walk or you'll have us in real trouble with broken bones."

"Be quiet!" he commanded her roughly, for he was discomforted by his awkwardness. She gave him a killing look but she made no answer to his rudeness, and presently they came around a curve and saw the market place at a little distance before them.

It was crowded with students, their black gowns flapping like crows' wings, and with country folk, staring at the students as they stood beside their stalls banked with flowers and vegetables. There were, besides, hawkers, crying their tawdry wares, and townsfolk, soberly dressed and moving with dignity among the stalls, baskets on their arms, their disdainful noses high in the air.

Dickon stopped at the outskirts of the square and looked the scene over. He wondered whether one place would be better than another for showing his tricks. Likely it wouldn't matter. This was as good a spot as any, or so it seemed to him, for people were streaming past him in plenty. If he could only catch their attention. . . .

He moved to one side and said to Cicely, "Stand a little apart from me and watch."

She went, obediently enough, almost as if the town and the people had turned her timid. He spread his cloak on the ground and took the golden balls from their bag and began to toss them into the air, higher and higher and higher. As he tossed he spoke, clear and loud, in a kind of rhythm as if he were speaking to music no one else could hear.

"Come," he intoned, "come and watch the golden

balls. Watch me catch them every time. Never a miss. Never a miss. Come and watch. Throw me a penny if you think me clever. Up, up, and up they go. Faster, faster, faster. They never fall. Never fall. Never touch ground. Up. Up. Up."

The sun caught the flying orbs and broke into splintered rays on their golden surfaces. At first nobody stopped to watch. Then, one curious man stood with his mouth open. He was joined quickly by another and another. Their intent bodies, and their eyes moving after the movement of Dickon's hands, drew others and in a few minutes, he had a semicircle of admirers with more behind them, pushing a little to get closer. He kept the balls flying over his head until his arms began to ache from the unaccustomed activity. Then, gracefully, he caught each one as it came to rest until he had all three held neatly, high above his head, between the fingers of one hand. The watchers clapped and Dickon bowed and threw his hat upon his spread cloak. At once a shower of coins fell into it and Dickon bowed again, this time very low as if he were in the presence of the Queen herself. Fools and gulls they may be, but these country people were not stingy with their money or with their appreciation. He felt curiously elated by their open-mouthed admiration for his skill.

Slowly, he put the golden balls back into their cover. The men and boys around him did not move. He picked up his hat and emptied the coins into the purse that hung at his waist and held up his hand. "My thanks, good people one and all," he said, loudly so all could hear, "for your approval of my skill. I should like to stay and show you more wonders."

He had palmed one of the coins as he put the others away and, while he had been talking, he had worked it in his palm until he was sure his muscles remembered their old cunning. Now he stretched out his hand to pluck the coin from the ear of the man nearest him. The crowd drew in its breath in a long gasp and Dickon said, "Ah! That one almost got away from me," and everyone guffawed. "And now, kind friends, farewell. I must be off to London."

He whipped the cloak from the ground, bundled it carelessly about his possessions, and turned to join Cicely, eager to show her the contents of his purse. He thought he could surely buy them all the food they wanted now.

Cicely was not there.

He had watched her when she had obeyed his order to move away from his pitch and had seen her take her stand at the edge of an alley's mouth where she could watch without seeming to be part of his act. She had smiled a little, a tight, disbelieving smile as if she expected him to make a fool of himself. He had put her and her doubts deliberately out of his mind so he could concentrate upon the juggling. But he had expected her to be there, waiting for him when he was done.

What had become of her? Had she gone off on her

own? Picking pockets of the unwary, no doubt. Very
well, if that was what she had done, she could get
along without him the rest of the way and good riddance. He jingled the coins in the purse. He could not,
likely, count on such good fortune in every market
place between here and London. He was well rid of
her. Then why didn't he feel lighthearted instead of
gloomy, almost sad, at the thought of losing her company?

He shrugged and started to go off in search of a stall
that sold food and heard a moan and a gasp. He followed the sound a little way into the alley and saw
Cicely pinned against a wall by two men. He dropped
his bundle and ran, lightly, to her and recognized her
tormentors as those she had called Jackdaw and Sparrow. Jackdaw's hand was moving toward her head as if
he would snatch away her hat. That would put the fat
in the fire!

Neither of the two men had heard Dickon come up,
being too much occupied with their sport. He grabbed
Jackdaw who was nearest by the back of his doublet and
spun the big, unsuspecting man about to face him.

"Here, now," Jackdaw said, "What's all this?"

"Leave my friend alone," Dickon said in a voice low
and tense with anger. He saw that Sparrow, surprised
at the interruption, had turned to see what was happening and he called to Cicely to run. She did as she
was told and disappeared into the deep shadows of the
lane. So far, so good. She'd likely be safe enough now.

Jackdaw was speaking and Dickon knew he had missed a part of what the big man was saying, ". . . mean the girl no harm. We were but. . . ."

Dickon did not wait to hear more. He could not, he guessed, fight both men at once. He'd best rid himself of this one now. He hit Jackdaw hard in the midriff and a part of his mind registered the look of surprise and hurt on the man's face as the breath whistled out of him and he clutched at his belly. Before he had a chance to get his breath back, Dickon hit him again, hard and straight on the jaw. Jackdaw fell heavily to the ground and lay there, making no effort to get up.

"You!"

Dickon whirled, panting, and saw Sparrow. He had been content to watch his friend make mincemeat of the slender lad who had dared challenge him and had braced himself against the wall the better to enjoy the fight in comfort. Time enough to go after the girl later. But when Dickon had knocked his huge opponent to the ground—and that with ease—Sparrow had hurled himself at Dickon and was almost on him when he spoke.

As Dickon turned he saw Sparrow's eyes red with anger. This was no bungler like Jackdaw but a skilled and dangerous fighter. There was no time to avoid the blow that was coming. Dickon twisted sideways to take it on his shoulder instead of his head. He heard cloth rip and felt a sting in his arm and saw the gleam of steel in Sparrow's hand. Why, the little shrimp had aimed to kill him. That one needed a lesson.

Sparrow's rush had taken him well beyond Dickon and, as the little man turned, he was off-balance. Dickon, angry in his turn, not heeding the blood staining his doublet, was after him in a second. He caught the hand that held the knife and twisted, hard, before Sparrow could properly regain balance. Sparrow bent and turned; kicked out at Dickon; tried in every way to writhe free, swearing mightily all the time. But Dickon, remembering Peter's lessons, held on, keeping his pressure on the thin wrist until, at last, the knife fell to the ground. Without taking his eyes off his opponent, Dickon picked up the knife and held it, point toward Sparrow's throat.

"So," Dickon said, "you'd fight an unarmed man with a knife. Now the tables are truly turned. Will you come on for more?"

"You—you. . . . Who do you think you are? Another Christopher Marlowe forever brawling, forever picking a fight?"

Dickon shook his head, not knowing whether he was hearing aright or not. What could this creature of the road know of Marlowe, the poet? Or was this some other man of like name who was a brawler and fighter? Before he could question the little man (who was rubbing his wrist and looking at Dickon as if he would learn every feature of his face by heart), Sparrow spoke again. "I'll pay you out for this, you villain. Just wait till I get to London. Argh, yes. I heard you tell those bumpkins you were bound there. I'll see you in the town. Never fear."

Jackdaw, recovering a little from the blow Dickon had used to fell him, put his hands behind him and pushed himself backward on his rump, slithering away from the two who glared at one another as if they might go at it again at any moment.

Sparrow spat at the place where Jackdaw had fallen and went on talking. "You just wait till my friends learn how you set upon me with my own knife. They'll help me find you if we have to search every bolt hole and thieve's warren in Londontown—find you and make you pay for your boldness. I'll have my revenge and it will be a good one I tell you."

Dickon's head felt suddenly full of wool ravelings. He was not aware of Jackdaw lifting himself now, to his knees. The shoulder wound though it was, he was sure, no more than a scratch, was hurting as if the devil himself had wielded the knife. His doublet was, likely, ruined, and now that the danger was past, he felt himself stupid with fatigue and the letdown after strain. Had Sparrow spoken Marlowe's name or had he not? If he had, would he know where the playmaker could be found? Better ask him. Scoundrel that he was, if he knew anything of Christopher Marlowe, Tom's Marlowe and Dickon's. . . .

"You," Dickon said, and looked where Sparrow had been standing. The place was empty. The little man had taken the few seconds when Dickon stood abstracted to run. There he was, dragging his lumbering friend after him, disappearing into the market crowds.

They'd be well lost before Dickon could be after them, he thought. No help for it. He wished he didn't feel so tired. He wished he could think clearly. He mustn't lose consciousness. He must pull himself together. If he didn't he'd never get to London. His hand felt heavy and he looked at it and found he was still holding the knife he'd taken from Sparrow. There was a little brownish-red stain on its edge. His blood, he realized, and felt a little sick and moved to lean against the windowless wall of the building that marked the lane's edge. He closed his eyes, willing his mind to steadiness. There was something he had to do. Someone. . . .

"*Dickon!* You were—were splendid! I saw the whole of it and you. . . . But, you're cut. Here. Sit down and let me look at your shoulder."

He opened his eyes and saw Cicely beside him, holding his hurt arm gently. What had come over the girl? This was a different Cicely, all concern and gentleness and shining-eyed admiration, as if he were a knight of olden times returning from the wars. He grinned at her and felt the sickness go from his stomach.

"It's not so much," he said. "The little devil did no more than scratch me. He's none so brave without his knife. And the big one's no fighter. Forget it and see what I got for my juggling." He started to reach for his purse and she stopped him.

"Now do as I say, Dickon," she ordered. "I reckon you've a full purse right enough, but I'll see your arm attended to before I feel the purse's weight. You're like a pig that's been stuck at killing time. Now sit down here while I get water from the fountain. You'll look a proper sight for staring eyes if you go on as you are."

Her talk was sensible and he knew it. He knew, too, he'd be better for a quiet moment. And his doublet was all streaked with bloodstains. He nodded and she left him, going quickly toward the market square. She was back in minutes with a battered cup full of water.

"Somebody left an old cup handy to the fountain," she explained as she washed the shallow cut on his shoulder. "Don't fear," she went on, seeing the look on his face. "I'll put it back." There was a flash of the old Cicely in her voice but it was soon gone. "There," she said, dabbing at the blood on his doublet, "that will have to serve. Better if I had a needle and thread to mend the rent in the cloth, but it's small and won't show much. You could have had it from a roadside bramble. For sure it won't attract the attention of the constable and have him after you asking questions thirteen to the dozen."

The constable! He was shocked again at his stupidity, for he'd given no thought to the fact he might have been taken up for fighting and bound over to keep the peace. Again he was in her debt and this time he was properly grateful.

"Thank you, Cicely," he said humbly. "I'd not even thought of the constable."

"No need for thanks," she said. "It's I should be

thanking you for—for saving me from those knaves. Oh, Dickon, I'm afraid Jackdaw saw through this disguise—or else he remembered my face from that long time ago. I—it may be I should not go with you, Dickon. They may come again, and both of them armed, and take you when you're not aware. To get at me, you know."

She broke off and shuddered, and he put out his hand and touched her awkwardly on the shoulder. Poor thing. She was as helpless as a babe new born, for all her brag and bluster earlier.

"Don't you be a ninny-hammer, Cicely," he said and shook her a little, gently. "We'll manage. Why those two are likely halfway to another place by now. To judge by the speed they were making through the market square when last I saw their backs, they'd no intention of waiting around for more."

"You *were* splendid, Dickon, and I'm sorry I made sport of you when we met. And I—I *could* manage, alone."

"Hush," he said, "and look." He took his purse and spread its contents on the ground and, together, they counted the coins. There was no great wealth here but there was enough to buy them food now and leave some over for future needs. He could not resist a boast and he said, "You see, I *can* make our way and without stealing either, as I promised you."

"Oh, Dickon," she said in a shaky voice. "I *said* I was sorry," and he felt small and mean for baiting her.

"Come," he said, "we must hurry."

She didn't move. "Rest awhile yet, Dickon. You need it."

"There's no *time*." He started to get up and felt dizzy and sat back down again.

"No time! No time!" she mocked him. "London will keep. Why must you hurry, hurry, hurry?"

He'd better explain, he thought. She'd lag and lag unless he gave her reasons for speed. Besides, he did need a little more time to recover his spent energy.

"There's a man in danger and I must get to him to warn him," he said.

"What man?" she asked and he sighed, thinking she would not be satisfied until she'd had the whole story.

He told her, then, all his story of Tom's dying and the final boon he'd asked of his younger brother. "The man's name is Christopher Marlowe," he ended.

"Christopher Marlowe?" her voice was blank.

"Yes. Christopher Marlowe, the maker of plays and the darling of all England."

"*I* never heard of him and I've stood in many an innyard to watch the players," she said stubbornly, as if she did not believe one word of what he was saying.

"You are, then, unfortunate," he said, irritated with her again. "He's likely the greatest man in the whole country."

"Pooh," she said. "And who's to say so?"

"You'd soon know for yourself how great he is if you'd ever listened to his verses. How I wish I could

hear my friend Robin Lang speaking some of his lines
this minute!

   'Is this the face that launched a thousand ships
   And burnt the topless towers of Ilium?
   Sweet Helen make me immortal with a kiss. . . .'

He was so lost in remembering the scene in *Dr. Faustus* that he had forgotten Cicely, though he seemed to
be staring straight at her. A slap on his face stung him
out of his reverie.

"You've no need to mock me," Cicely said, "with
your talk of faces launching ships and burning towers.
Calling me 'Helen' too. I know I'm no beautiful thing
as I stand in these—these rags and my face all dirty to
boot. B—b—but it's cruel to—to. . . ."

"Whatever are you talking about?" he interrupted
her. "I made no mock of you, silly goose. Oh!"

He laughed, and seeing his laughter only increased
her hurt and anger, he added, "Cicely, Cicely, I was
only speaking lines from a play by that same Christopher Marlowe, a play called *The Tragical History of
Dr. Faustus*. All London's talking of it and I saw it
played at Cambridge just a month ago. I did not
mean. . . ."

She sniffed and looked at him and, suddenly, was
laughing at herself. "I *was* a silly goose," she said.

He got up and found he was steady enough on his
feet and in his head now. He gave her a little shake
and said, "Let's be on our way. We'll find an inn and

fill our stomachs. The sun's at the noonstead and I'm as hungry as that poor starveling bear we passed on the road. As you must be."

"Oho!" she said, her eyes sparkling with mischief, "Have you so soon forgot you'll have no dealing with a thief?" She picked up the empty cup and shook it in front of his face. "And that's what you'll make of me if we don't return this. Or shall I keep it after all? It might fetch a groat in thieve's market."

She was laughing at him again and he was in no mood for her banter. He felt empty and exhausted after the excitement of the morning. "Put it back, then, and be quick about it," he said roughly. "Or here. Give it to me. I'll drop it at the fountain as we pass, for there's the Sign of the Fighting Bull showing just beyond, and there I have no doubt we can find food."

CHAPTER VII

The Fighting Bull

As they came near the inn door, Cicely began to walk more and more slowly until she was lagging several steps behind Dickon. He said, over his shoulder, "Do hurry up Ci," and remembered there were people about and he must not call her name and changed what he was saying to, "Slow-back, or we'll never be fed."

"Wait," she called, forgetting in her turn to keep her tongue still, and he shook his head at her and looked about to see if anyone had noticed. So far as he could tell no one had, and he waited for her to come up to him. She came close and spoke softly in his ear. "Go ahead and find places for us. I—I can't go in there as I am, all disheveled where those oafs pulled my clothes about and about."

He stared at her for a second then burst out laughing.

"Very well, *my lady,*" he whispered back. "Go and

make yourself beautiful. But see you keep that hat on your head and your mouth tight shut."

She went away toward the innyard and the pump that would be there. He watched her go, still smiling at her womanly concern for her looks even in the ragamuffin's clothes she was wearing. He noticed she moved with grace, with beauty even, not like a hoyden of the road, lumpish and awkward. He wondered whether there might be something in her claim to high birth. Forsooth, there were tales aplenty of babies stolen away or strayed from their homes and never heard of again. He reckoned he'd likely never know. Nor would she, poor girl. He lifted his shoulders dismissing idle speculation, and pushed open the door of The Fighting Bull.

The deep shadows of the common room blinded him after the bright noonday sun outside and he stood with his back to the door, waiting for his eyes to adjust to the changed light. He could not, at first, believe his ears when he heard, or thought he heard, his own name called in this place of strangers. He shook his head to clear it, thinking himself perhaps still mazed from his morning's efforts. But, there it was again.

"Dickon! Dickon Fontayne!"

He started to examine the room and felt his shoulders seized from behind and himself spun about, and he found himself staring at a tall, handsome young man dressed point-device, though in the conservative fashion, not like the fop he'd seen on the road. He was grinning as if his face would split in two and pummeling Dickon between the shoulders, as if his very life depended upon it. For several heartbeats Dickon failed to recognize him, then, not really believing what he saw, he spoke as if he were part of a miracle.

"Robin Lang! It can't be. But—but. . . ."

"It is!" Robin finished triumphantly. "Dickon, Dickon, what do you here? Surely you've not forsaken our Cambridge for this—this. . . . Faith! it's good to see you, Dickon. Come over here where we can talk."

Without waiting for agreement, he took Dickon's arm and dragged him toward a table set beneath a window where a man who wore distinction like a cloak already sat. Dickon was suddenly conscious of his own crumpled hose and torn, stained doublet. He wished he, too, had betaken himself to the pump before he came into the inn. The thought reminded him of Cicely and he looked behind him, but she had not yet come inside. He tried to hang back, to explain about his companion, but Robin, in his old, remembered, headlong way, was paying no attention; was not, indeed, hearing anything but the words tumbling and rattling from his own mouth.

". . . and so," he was saying, "the plague adds another notch to its tale of death—*and* a big one, for our Lord Admiral's Company is gone and done for, split into a handful of ex-actors, most of them, poor devils, forced to take to the road and beg their way back to London having nothing left but the clothes they stand up in. Me—I was lucky, for I only had to tell my father and he, bless his generous heart and full purse, sent me enough and to spare to get me to London and a new start. So here we are and here is Ned Alleyn, Dickon, the finest actor in all England—nay, in all the world—and my friend. *He'll* never need to beg his bread, for there's not a company of players in the land would not want him with them."

The man at the table had risen and made a deep bow to Dickon. "Sit with us," he said, indicating the chair beside him, "and pay no heed to Robin's prattle. He's often talked of you, Dickon Fontayne, remembering the days before the playhouse called him away from his studies."

Ned Alleyn's voice had the depth and range and power of the organ in Queen's College Chapel that Dickon had loved to listen to in winter twilights when the music master had, sometimes, played for his own pleasure. Dickon felt himself embraced by that voice and found himself recalling the plays he'd seen at Cambridge, wishing he could be in the pit of some theater hearing Alleyn speaking lines written by Christopher Marlowe or even by the new, young playmaker one of the masters at Cambridge had spoken of—this Will Shakespeare from his own Cotswold country. Suddenly shy, Dickon heard his own voice shaking as he thanked Alleyn for his invitation and took the seat indicated.

"So!" Robin said when they were all seated and Alleyn had called a serving man to bring another flagon of ale, "So, what of you, Dickon? What are you doing in Oxford?"

"Nothing but passing through it on my way to London. Tom. . . ." He hesitated a second to gulp back the feeling of loneliness and loss the saying of Tom's name brought into his throat—"Tom is dead."

"How? When?" Robin asked.

"A week ago. Of an illness he took upon a journey." Dickon knew he couldn't talk of Tom without blubbering like a child and he turned away from the subject quickly, before Robin could offer his sympathy. "It's that brings me to Oxford and, in time, to London."

"Tom had business in London?" Robin asked.

"No," Dickon said, "not, at least, business of his own. He sent me to warn Christopher Marlowe, for Tom believed him to be in danger of his life."

Alleyn, after his first greeting had withdrawn himself a little from the other two, as if he would leave them to their reunion without interference from another. His clear, gray eyes that seemed to have a secret power of their own, were half-closed, and he was as still as if he were sunk in quiet sleep. But he was listening, and when Dickon spoke Marlowe's name, his eyes flew open and in another second he sat straight in his chair and said, "Marlowe! Do you mean Kit Marlowe of London?"

Dickon almost choked on his words, jerked back from what he was saying to sudden remembrance of Alleyn's presence. "Yes. Yes, Master Alleyn. My brother was friend to Christopher Marlowe when they were both studying at Cambridge. Do you, too, know him then?"

Robin chuckled. "There," he said, "there speaks the Cambridge scholar, Ned. So lost in his studies he might as well be locked up in some tower of ivory, forgetful of all the world about him. I'll warrant, Dickon, you've not been inside a playhouse since I left you, for all we used to sneak our way into any play we could hear of; yes, and take parts in some few as well."

Dickon shook his head and would have explained he had missed no chance to see any cry of players who came to Cambridge or near it. Robin gave him no time to say his say. "Look you, Dickon," he rattled on, "I told you our Ned Alleyn is the greatest actor in the world. Until now he's been, as I have been, with the Lord Admiral's Company. Marlowe wrote plays for that same company and Ned has brought Kit Marlowe's characters to stages all over London, not to mention many towns in the rest of England. To the groundlings he *is* Tamburlaine or Dr. Faustus or Barabbas in *The Jew of Malta*. Never was there such acting. Not. . . ."

"Have done, Robin," Alleyn said quietly. "You can talk of all this another time. Your point is, I don't doubt, made to Dickon—that I do indeed know Christopher Marlowe and hold him in good esteem. Now, I'd like to hear more of this quest your friend has undertaken and I haven't much time for listening. You know I must make haste to Bath if I'm to take my place with Lord Strange's Men. Now, Dickon, you were saying your brother sent you to London to find Kit Marlowe and warn him. Why?"

Dickon explained about Tom's wait at Dover, about what Tom had overheard, and his fears for his old friend. Alleyn's face grew more concerned as Dickon talked and when he was done, the actor struck the table with doubled fist so hard the flagons jumped.

"By my faith!" he said. "Your brother was right, I am afraid. Marlowe is not one to run from trouble or guard his back in time of danger. He'll likely pay small heed to your warning, Dickon, but find him you must and warn him you must. And you may add my word to your brother's."

"But why should he be in danger, Ned?" Robin asked. "Who in all England would want to harm the foremost playmaker in—in all the world? Everyone must love him if only for the pleasure he brings them."

"Robin, Robin," Alleyn said. "I see you, too, have an ivory tower for a dwelling place. There are many Marlowes, not just Marlowe the playmaker."

"But," Robin persisted, "I've heard you speak often of his wisdom and his kindness. How could such things make enemies for him?"

Alleyn said, slowly, "Indeed, his friends think him wise and kind, generous and always good company. There's no better companion for passing an hour in an alehouse. No better mind for exploring a new thought or arguing an old one. And there's no better friend to have at your side in trouble. But all men are not Marlowe's friends."

"But—but," Robin's face wore a bewildered look.

"Those other Marlowes, Robin, are not so popular. Kit's quick to take offense and quick to draw a dagger in his own behalf or another's. He has already been taken up and lodged in jail for brawling. Oh, he was quit of the charge right enough, but such mud sticks. Then there is the matter of his student days at Cambridge."

Robin said, "The Queen's business, you mean. Dickon. . . ."

Dickon said quickly, "If you mean the interference of the Queen's council in the matter of his degree, I know of that for Tom told me. But I don't understand it." He looked at Alleyn and directed the question to him. "I don't understand how Cambridge scholars like Master Marlowe and my brother—for Tom had a part in that business at Rheims—are allowed to be spies."

Alleyn didn't answer at once. He seemed off in some secret place in his own mind. Robin said, smiling a little, "But there's no dishonor in the Queen's business, Dickon. It's said many gentlemen scholars, writers, even courtiers go to spy out trouble that might threaten the Queen's person or England. Besides that's an old, old story now."

Alleyn shook himself and came out of his study. "Maybe not so old, Robin. Marlowe has been—I'm sure of it, though he would never speak of it—on the

Queen's business again and that not long ago. He went
to Scotland just after Christmas when rumor ran that
some of the Scots, still smarting at the death of their
Queen Mary and always looking for ways to bring popery back to this land, were conspiring with Philip of
Spain to put *him* on Gloriana's throne. Thank the
heavens that snake was scotched in time."

"I still don't see why Marlowe should be in danger
now," Dickon said. He felt, without knowing just why,
that he must come to some comprehension of all these
different Marlowes if he were to try to save the man.

"Because, Dickon, those who go upon secret business
of the Queen walk always in danger. This spying
makes strange bedfellows. Sir Francis Walsingham
used whatever tools came to his hand and not all of
them were the gentlemen and scholars Robin spoke of.
And such a man may learn a thousand things dangerous to other men—even to men in high places.
Usually there's no need to talk of such things. But
mark you. These are not ordinary times. There's been a
deal of trouble in London. A letter from my
mouse."

"Your *mouse!*" Dickon couldn't keep back the ejacu-
lation. Letters from a mouse!

Alleyn looked embarrassed for a moment before he
said, "I do beg your pardon. It's a—a sort of pet
name for my wife and it slipped from my tongue. At any
rate, I had a letter from her yesterday telling of what
has been happening in the town. There is a man, she

says, a scribbler named Thomas Kyd." The scorn in Alleyn's voice as he spoke of Kyd was searing. "This Kyd is suspected of trouble-making. He's in prison and, I'm afraid, has no love for Kit; for, being a half-baked playmaker himself, he is jealous of the greater man."

"What can a scribbler do, Ned?" Robin asked. "How can he who is of such small account bring harm to Kit?"

"There was a time when Kyd and Marlowe shared a lodging in London and, when Kyd was taken and his rooms searched in the usual way, the searchers discovered a paper of an atheistical nature. Kyd, so my mou —my wife writes me, said upon his oath the paper belonged to Kit and was somehow left behind when he changed his lodgings."

"Oh!" Robin said. "So the old lie comes again."

"What has atheism to do with all this?" Dickon asked. "It's only an idea."

"Only an idea," Alleyn repeated slowly. "True enough. But, Dickon Fontayne, ideas can, in themselves, be dangerous. If it can be proven that Christopher Marlowe is in truth an atheist, it follows to the common mind, he is then a danger to the State. For the State is ordained of God for the governing of men, and if there is no God, there is then no properly sanctioned State. To deny the very foundation upon which the State rests is treason. And treason is punishable by death. Dickon, Dickon," he went on seeing the disbelief in Dickon's face, "it is, I see, as Robin says, you are a scholar and withdrawn from the ordinary ways of the world. I doubt you can begin to understand the disordered thinking, the superstitious fears of the ordinary man."

Dickon said, stubbornly, "No man can make me believe Christopher Marlowe is a danger to the State. Have you not just said he is likely still upon the Queen's business? *Or* that he is an atheist. He is just *thinking*. Thinking all sides of the question. I'm sure of that."

"His friends know it, Dickon," Alleyn said. "But a man who does not fear to say what he thinks can make many enemies. So it is with Marlowe. Some men hate him for they fear his very ideas, knowing the power of thought can change a world."

He stopped and sat quietly as if he would give Dickon the chance to consider a little what he had been saying. Nor did Dickon or Robin break the pool of silence, which seemed to encircle their table and cut them off from the babble of noise in the room, as if it had been a wall too thick to admit sound.

At last Alleyn gave himself a little shake and smiled at the other two and said, "But look you, lads, enough of this talk. What is important now is for you both to understand the council *must* consider this charge of atheism cast by Kyd—or seem to consider it. And they have commanded Marlowe, so my wife writes me, to hold myself ready to come before them—daily if sent for—until they are ready to examine him."

"Ho!" Robin said. "It's none so bad then, for if they had any serious doubts of him, they would have put him in Clink prison straightaway."

"There's that," Alleyn agreed and thought for a space. "But it may be he would be safer in the Clink. For it's not the council's action that frets me. Look you. Suppose—just suppose Marlowe has some knowledge from the past that might endanger one of those strange bedfellows I spoke of. Further, suppose this man knows this and reasons that Marlowe, when he comes before the Council, will tell all he knows to save himself the rack—as yon Kyd did. Now what would you do, if you had the chance, if you were such a person?"

"Eliminate the danger to myself," Robin said promptly.

"But—but such a man as Master Marlowe would never do such a thing!" Dickon protested almost in the same breath.

Alleyn said, sounding more serious than he had before, "Who can say what any man might reveal in the face of such a threat as the rack? I would not trust myself, I can tell you."

He was quiet for a moment, thinking of the torture, and he shivered a little before he went on, "Now do you see, lads, why I feel there is danger—*real* danger for Marlowe? It's important for you to get to London as fast as possible. Would to heaven I could go with you and pound some sense into Kit Marlowe's head.

Since I can't—well, you must be my emissaries as well as Tom Fontayne's, rest his soul. Now, Dickon, what money have you for the journey?"

Dickon bristled. He hated to admit to this splendid gentleman that his fortune extended no further than the few coins he had collected this very day. What business was it of Alleyn's how heavy his purse was? To answer the question seemed, in some hidden way, to show Tom in a poor light, and that he would not do. But the man was waiting. "Ah-h-h, u-m-m," he said, trying to find a way to tell Alleyn this was none of his business and to tell him without discourtesy, for he had no wish to insult Robin's friend.

"Well, Dickon?" Alleyn pushed him. "Have you enough silver to hire horses and a room at an inn and the like?"

"There—there isn't very much silver," Dickon said and emptied his slim purse on the table for Alleyn to see.

"By all the saints there is not!" Alleyn exclaimed.

"But I can always get more," Dickon said and added with pride, "I'm a juggler and a good one."

"Ho!" Alleyn said and added quickly, "I'm sorry, lad. I'm sure you could make your own way. And I know I have no right to inquire into the weight of your purse. But don't you understand? You must go quickly with your warning, and if you have to make your way on foot, stopping to earn your bread as you go, you can make no haste. Here," he brought his hand from under the table and, after a quick look around him to be sure they were not overlooked, added several gold coins to the pennies on the table.

Dickon stared at the heap of winking gold, not touching it.

"Put it up quickly, Dickon," Alleyn said. "Don't leave it where any thief may see it and plan to waylay you for it. Men have been killed and left in ditches for less."

"But—but," Dickon said, "I—I can't take this from you—a stranger just met."

Alleyn scrabbled the coins together and put them back in the purse and thrust the purse at Dickon. "Look you, Dickon Fontayne," he said. "These coins are not for you. They are for my friend Christopher Marlowe. Robin will tell you I'm no poor, struggling actor but a man of some wealth. And I would give it all, if need be, to save a friend from danger. There are few men like Christopher Marlowe among the catchpenny writers of this day, and England can ill afford to lose him. Keep your pride for a better occasion."

Dickon, still reluctant, took up the purse, much heavier now, and returned it to its place. Alleyn nodded and went on with his talk.

"Now, we must plan quickly. So soon as you have eaten you're to take horses and ride as quickly as you may to London. When you get into the town you are to go at once to my wife."

He broke off and looked about him and, catching the eye of a servant, summoned him and told him to bring paper and a quill and an inkpot together with the reckoning. "I'll send her a note and she will help you. I don't know just where Marlowe is lodging at this present, for it's not likely he'll be found in his usual place with London so full of the plague."

Dickon leaned closer to the actor and said softly, "Master Alleyn. I—I have this." He pulled his jewel from beneath his ruff and showed it to Alleyn. "I believe the jewel is of some value. It belonged to my mother. There were reasons why I couldn't change the ring for coins before I left. I should like to give it to you in exchange for the gold."

Alleyn's face softened and he left off the nervous drumming upon the table he'd taken up when the servant went to do his bidding. "You're a good lad, Dickon Fontayne," he said. "But keep your jewel." He glanced at the ring and motioned Dickon to return it to its place. "That looks to be a fine bauble, lad, and you will, likely, need it when you come to London. I'll tell my wife to see you get a fair price for it. Remember, you are not in my debt. Just keep always in your mind that what I do, I do for my friend and do not fret about it."

The servant came then with the things Alleyn had sent for and the actor scribbled busily for a time, waved the paper in the air to dry the ink, then folded the note, and added a superscription. He started to hand the paper to Robin and changed his mind and gave it instead to Dickon. Robin grinned and Dickon felt, suddenly, taller for Alleyn's trust.

"And now," Alleyn said, "I must be off. Robin will help you, Dickon. God be with you both and bring you quickly to Christopher Marlowe."

When he had gone Robin said, "Well, Dickon Fontayne, let us. . . ."

He stopped for Dickon had half risen. Watching Alleyn's departure, he'd seen Cicely standing in the doorway. While they had been talking of Marlowe and his danger, he had forgotten her completely. Now she looked so small, so uncertain of herself, so out of place in this room filled with burly men, he felt his throat tighten with pity for her. He pushed back his chair and started to her rescue.

She saw him almost at once and moved toward him through the crowd, her face showing relief at finding him. He took her arm as she came up to him and led her to the table, not trying to talk amidst the clamor about them except to bend close to her and whisper a reminder that she must not speak before Robin. As they reached the table Robin said, "Well, who is *this,* Dickon?"

"A friend of the road," Dickon said. "We met only this morning—by chance." (He'd not tell Robin the chance had been an attempt at highway robbery. He'd have to think of a reason for Cicely's silence.) "We decided to keep one another company on the road to London."

"Now that's a complication," Robin said and looked as if a sudden cloud had shadowed his normally cheer-

ful face. Dickon wondered if the old friend could possibly resent the new one.

"Not at all," he said stiffly, and Robin frowned at
him. Dickon turned to Cicely and motioned her to the
chair Alleyn had vacated. She sat, a little reluctantly,
watching Robin's face.

"I suggest we have some food before we consider
further plans," Dickon said stiffly and summoned the
potboy with a grand gesture.

CHAPTER VIII

The Problem of Cicely

"And now—what about the—ah—*lady*?" Robin asked when they had eaten.

The breath went out of Dickon in a whoosh as if his friend had suddenly turned on him and struck him.

"The—the———" he began and Robin stared at him as if he had gone witless and said, "Come now, Dickon. Did you take me for a fool *and* a blind one, to think I'd not see through that—that ridiculous attempt at a disguise?"

He waved his hand at Cicely.

"Here now, you," she began furiously. She was glad the need to keep her teeth clenched against speaking was over, but this Robin had no right to be making such remarks about her. She'd done the best she could, and the disguise had served well enough till now. Except of course, for the unfortunate meeting with Jackdaw who had seen her face before.

"You've no cause. . . ."

"Be quiet, Cicely," Dickon ordered. He turned to Robin to ask, "How—how did you know?"

Robin gave a short bark of a laugh before he answered. "By her walk. By the way she stands and sits. By a certain—certain *softness* of features that never belonged to a proper man. You can't be a man of the theater so long as I have, Dickon, and not know these things. Why, observation of such details is half the fight in learning to be an actor. Of course, it's no business of mine if you wish to dress your—your light o' love in men's clothes. It's only. . . ."

"ROBIN!" Dickon was on his feet in outrage, his fists clenched, anger bristling his hair till it stood out from his head like a fighting hound's.

Robin said, hastily, "Now, Dickon. I meant no harm and I do beg you—*and* the lady—to pardon me if I'm wrong. By the look of it. . . ."

"The look of it," Dickon shouted. "You—you should know me better, Robin Lang. You. . . ."

"Let be, Dickon," Cicely said quietly. She was a little amused by his anger, and a little pleased. "Your friend was mistaken and has said so. He has asked your pardon and mine. Cool your anger and be sensible. If it be true I am so easily seen to be womanish we'd best decide what's to be done and waste no time in idle quarrels. Who's to say we may not meet other players upon the road?"

"She's right, you know, Dickon," Robin said. "I am sorry if I misread the signs. Now sit down and compose yourself, and tell me how you come to have in your company this girl masquerading as a—a scare-crow."

Dickon, still crimson of face with anger and injured dignity, showed no sign of taking Robin's advice. Cicely reached out and caught him by the doublet and gave it such a tug he was forced back into his chair so hard he bounced a little. "Be sensible, Dickon Fontayne," she said. "You've no time for anger if you're to find this precious Marlowe and warn him of his danger."

Robin said, "Dickon?" and when Dickon didn't answer laid a hand on his arm. "Do give over, Dickon. Cicely's right. We can make a fight of it later, if you still wish, but now we should get on with our business."

Dickon, even with so little time to think, had realized he'd been overhasty in anger. It was true what Robin had said. He *had* laid himself and Cicely open to Robin's charge. They'd thought she could pass for a man and no questions asked, so long as she kept her mouth shut. They hadn't, for a moment, considered her disguise would be so inadequate as it evidently was. Nor could he now, thinking back over the last few minutes, see why he had been so quickly angered at Robin's slur upon Cicely's honor. What could have got into him? Anger at his close and only friend! That was absurd. Cicely's honor could take care of itself. It was not his responsibility.

He smiled at Robin. "I'm sure you meant no harm

and spoke only of what you saw—or thought you saw. We won't fight, Robin."

"Now, the saints be praised," Cicely said and looked so droll in her relief that the last of the tension went out of the room. Robin, for no very good reason Dickon could see, began to laugh and in very short order the others were laughing with him in great, cheerful shouts.

When they sobered, Robin said, "You'd better explain about Cicely, Dickon. And while you're about it you'd as well throw in the fight you must have had on the road, for I'll warrant that rent in your doublet was made by a dagger thrust."

Dickon drew in his breath and let it out in a long sigh. It seemed to him he'd spent eons of time explaining himself this day.

Robin said, "Is it so hard a task, then? But then you were never one for much talking." He laughed shortly and leaned over to dig his fist into Dickon's ribs.

Dickon grinned and began his story. When he spoke of Cicely's attempt at highway robbery, Robin got part way out of his seat and sketched her a bow and said, "My compliments on your courage, Mistress, if not on your wisdom." Cicely made a face at him and in that moment she did look like a young boy being teased. But when Dickon came to tell of Cicely's life on the road, Robin's mobile face sobered and grew almost sad. And when Dickon was done, Robin turned to Cicely and said, "We'll see you to London, Dickon and

I, and see your safely settled there. Failing all else, I'll take you to my mother who never yet turned her back upon any creature in distress. Now, Dickon, what of this fight you were in?"

Dickon sketched as rapidly as he could the outlines of his encounter with Jackdaw and Sparrow.

"Ho!" Robin said, eyes lifting with pleasure, "I'd forgotten what a scrapper you can be, when necessary. I wish I had been there. Just let those two come around again and we'll give them another taste of defeat, eh Dickon?"

Dickon nodded. He had no wish for another fight and he hoped he'd seen the last of the loathsome Sparrow. Besides he didn't know what kind of fighter Robin would be against such a man as Sparrow. He said, "In any case, Robin, we'd better be on our way. Call up the servant and let's pay the reckoning."

"You go too fast, Dickon," Robin said. "You'd look a proper fool coming to The Stag at Windsor, where we'll likely stay this night, in a doublet, knife-slashed and still stained with your blood. Likely you've another in your pack?"

Dickon shook his head.

"Then you must make do with one of mine unless Cicely here can mend it." Cicely nodded.

"And what about Cicely?" Robin went on. "She would, maybe, do well enough, on the road, in what she's wearing if the two of us were to keep her always between us with fists and knives ready for any who might challenge her 'manhood.' But she'll make a sorry figure in those rags coming riding into Windsor as she will be doing."

Cicely said, "You can stop thinking about me, Robin Lang. You and Dickon can get on with your ridiculous questing after warning a man who, like as not, doesn't need to be warned. All this talk of danger and hurry! I'll do very well by myself while the two of you go riding after moonshine worries."

Dickon was distressed by her words. He thought they were no more than bravado born of self-pity. Just the same he wanted to comfort her and reached his hand to her and said, "Don't worry, Cicely. You well know I'll not desert you, for I promised," and was surprised to hear the softness and warm concern in his own voice.

To his horror he saw tears making her blue eyes milky. What had he done? He was only trying to reassure her. He looked at Robin.

Robin winked at him and said to Cicely, making his voice harsh, "Stop your sniveling, wench, and give your mind to thinking. I told you we'd see you safe to London and settled and that's an end of it."

Dickon said, "Robin!" thinking to reprimand his harshness and stopped in mid-thought.

Cicely's tears were gone. She sat straight in her chair and lifted her head and looked at Robin as if she would like to box his ears. "You, you villain!" she said. "I'm not a sniveling wench and you've no cause to call me so."

Dickon thought he'd never, if he lived a thousand

years, understand people. How had Robin known
Cicely needed harshness to stop her crying?

Robin said, "Now that's better spirited. So, we can
get on now with what we must decide before we move
one step."

"What? What's to decide?" she asked, sullen still.

"Just this. Do you travel as lass or lad? Which shall
it be?"

"Lass," Cicely said promptly. "I'm fair weary of
men's dress."

"Lad!" Dickon disagreed. "You'll be safer so,
Cicely."

"Lad!" Robin said. "Dickon's right, you know, and
it will be only a day or two more. Besides, I can easily
find you proper lad's clothes for I've dealt before,
when we were playing here and lacked some oddment
of dress, with an old fellow who has old clothes—but
men's clothes only, mind you—to sell, and some of
them good enough for a lordling. But the devil knows
where we'd find you woman's dress, short of calling on
a mantua-maker and waiting upon her skill to fashion
what you wish. And that we've no time for, if I'm to
judge by the pother about my sisters' dresses or my
mother's. So, lad it must be."

Cicely sighed. "Very well," she agreed, "but it's
hard."

Dickon frowned. "But what will we do about her
hair, Robin? If we'll be sleeping at an inn she cannot
forever be wearing a hat."

"Cut it off," Robin said matter-of-factly.

"No! Oh, no," Cicely said. "You shall not cut off my hair."

"Oho! The lady's vain." Robin laughed. "But cut it we will, Mistress; for, once again, our Dickon's right. And it's not only the question of wearing your hat to bed, if it be the inn's crowded and we are forced to the common room, which I do promise you is no place for an obvious lady. One good high wind upon the road and, whisk! Off with your hat and, likely, down with your hair and your masquerade's discovered for all to see. Then would the fat be in the fire! No, Cicely, the hair must go. It's bad enough that every move you make is likely to give away your womanhood." He waited a minute, examining her as if she had been a prize sheep. "Still, you're small and, in proper clothes with your hair gone, we can pretend to any yokel who looks at you slaunchwise and wondering, that you're still in your first youth. You'll be our younger—our *much* younger—brother. And it could just be true that most eyes would be less sharp to discover you than mine. For I played, for a time, the women's parts in the company and so had to learn how to pretend in walking and standing, to be a woman. In any case you've no need to fret, girl. We'll cut only so much of your hair as we must and it will grow again and quickly."

Cicely looked as if she were about to cry again. Dickon said, "So, that's settled. Now, will you call for the reckoning and let us get on with it? Oh!"

"What now?" Robin asked.

"We can hardly shear away Cicely's hair here in the common room!"

Robin had already summoned the servant and was doling out coins to pay for their food. He waited until the man had gone, threading his way among the crowd that threatened to burst the very walls of the inn now, before he answered. "Dickon, Dickon," he said, "I do believe you're learning at last to take thought to the practical things of this life. And none too soon. We'll go abovestairs for the shearing, of course."

"Will you stop talking of me as if I were a sheep?" Cicely put in.

Robin ignored her. "Alleyn and I were fortunate," he said. "We were able to secure for ourselves a private chamber with a parlor attached so we should not have to bed with the rabble and likely have all our belongings searched for hidden treasure, if we didn't get a knife in our ribs into the bargain. Come, I'll take you there where you'll be safe enough from prying eyes while I go to the clothes seller, and beg the loan of a pair of shea—scissors from the housemaid."

An hour later they were on their way, refreshed and spruced. Robin had sent a little maid to them with hot water for washing and, while Dickon cleansed his face and hands, Cicely mended the rent in his doublet with needle and thread she'd begged of the maid. She sponged away the remains of the blood and found a brush Robin used for his hair and brushed Dickon's clothes until they were neat and clean. Dickon was dressed again and presentable by the time Robin returned with a fine doublet and hose and a cloak and hat, that must have belonged to a very small scholar at one of Oxford's colleges.

Cicely held them against her and nodded. "They'll fit well enough," she said and went to the other room where she made quick work of her changing. She came then to stand in the parlor doorway, dropping the filthy, old garments on the floor beside her. She had brushed her own hair to shining and left it falling in soft waves almost to her waist.

Dickon stared at her. The new clothes transformed her from bobtail hoyden and let her fine bones and her neat, elegant figure show.

Robin said, "By all the saints, my lady, clothes do make the man—or the boy—if they are well-fitting and clean. Now we'll finish the transformation."

He picked up the scissors and beckoned Cicely closer. She made no move to go to him. "Please," she begged in a very little voice, "*please* let me keep my hair? I will wrap it close about my head and pull the hat so well down upon it no wind will blow it off." She looked at Dickon. "Please, Dickon."

Dickon said, "I don't see why we have to cut it, Robin." He felt he couldn't bear to see that halo shorn away.

"Don't be stupid!" Robin was irritated at all this fuss about a little hair-cutting. "You have yourself said it. The girl can't sleep in her hat. We're likely to have problems enough on the way without adding one that isn't necessary. Be sensible, girl, and come here. Else I'll have to—to tie you since I doubt Dickon will hold you for me. And that will make the cutting harder and I'll likely bungle it. Come now."

Cicely looked from one to the other. Dickon turned away from her, but Robin kept his brown, steady eyes upon her and she knew he wouldn't weaken. She thought of leaving them and keeping her hair but she knew she wouldn't get far alone, and she didn't know where else to look for help. She lifted her chin and walked to the chair Robin indicated and sat in it, forcing herself to pretend to calm. Her hair would grow again, no doubt. In time. But it was, it had always been, the one thing she could take pride in through the long and often brutal years upon the road. She'd borne the laughter and taunts every week, when, wherever she was, she had lugged water from the nearest stream to wash it. Losing it now, on top of the other trials laid upon her in this week of trials, was too much. But, it seemed, there was nothing she could do about it.

She closed her eyes as Robin laid the scissors against the first of the tresses, and felt as if it were her head he was about to cut off. But, when he had finished and rummaged in his portmanteau and found a mirror and held it for her, she had to agree the face that looked back at her from massed curls, tight now the heavy pull of the long hair had been removed, did indeed give her more the look of a boy. The new look amused her a little and she found she could manage a wan smile at her own image.

Robin said, *"Now,* what's to do with *that?"* and pointed to the mass of hair on the floor. Cicely automatically turned to see what he meant and gasped and turned her back and went quickly into the other room so she would not have to look again.

Dickon said, "We can't just leave it there. Or the old clothes either. Couldn't we stuff it all behind the bed?"

"Better not," Robin said. "This inn is one of Ned's favorites and if we left such a mess behind he'd surely be blamed for it and made less welcome when he comes again. No, better bundle it all together as best we can and stuff it in my saddlebags until we can find a place upon the road to bestow it under leaves and such trash."

They scratched together the hair and hid it in the midst of the discarded clothes before they called to Cicely and, dividing Robin's boxes and bags between them, went to the stableyard to bespeak horses for themselves. They were fair enough mounts and looked rested and Dickon felt his spirits rising, thinking their troubles were surely over for the time at least.

But it was not to be so. "You can ride, of course, Cicely," he said and she answered, "Well enough, though I'm more accustomed to walking. But you'll have to help me mount for those are great, tall creatures."

Dickon groaned in his mind though he was careful

not to let the sound come through his lips. It did not
seem to occur to Cicely it would look a queer thing for
a young lad to be helped to mount a horse. He glanced
quickly about the stableyard. It was almost deserted,
but one or two stableboys were lounging against the
wall, watching all they did. He muttered to Robin,
"Cicely can't mount alone. Cover us while I get her
up."

Robin glanced up from checking his saddle. He
looked startled, even unbelieving, for an instant. Then
he nodded and moved his horse so as to block Cicely's
from the stable. Dickon put his hand under Cicely's
boot and lifted her quickly toward the saddle. For a
minute he was afraid she was going to overbalance and
pitch off on the other side of the beast. But she caught
herself and steadied and turned to make another face
at Robin who was, once more, laughing at her. "Can I
help it that I'm not a great lout like you and your
Robin?" she muttered to Dickon as he settled himself
in the saddle of the third horse.

"Never mind," he said, and led the way out of the
stableyard and into the high street. He hoped with all
his mind he'd never see this town again.

CHAPTER IX

The Posting House

They didn't reach Windsor that night. The sun had been more than halfway to setting before they were finally away from Oxford. And, although Robin had taken the lead and set a fast pace at first, it soon became clear that Cicely was, indeed, more used to walking than to riding. She said nothing, determined to give Robin and Dickon no further cause for complaint of her. But they had gone no more than ten miles when her legs, aching from the unaccustomed need to grip the horse's flanks, and her backside, already saddle-sore, forced a groan from her.

Robin paid no attention if, indeed, he heard the small sound. But Dickon heard and reined his horse to a walk and came back to her.

"What is it, Cicely?" he asked. "Are you ill?"

"It's—it's nothing, Dickon." But she could not keep her knees taut a moment longer or her shoulders straight. Glad for the small relief, her body slumped in the saddle in spite of her effort to keep it erect. She leaned forward pretending to stroke the head of the great brute she rode, hoping to cover her distress and the weariness in all her bones so Dickon would not see her state.

But Dickon, watching her, read the signs and guessed their cause. "How long has it been since you were last upon a horse's back?" he asked.

"Let be, Dickon," she begged. "I'll do well enough."

"Answer me, Cicely!"

"I—I cannot say rightly. Horses—in the mind of him who was my master—were for stealing and selling, not for riding. One summer—seven years ago or it may be eight—she who called herself my mother was taken ill and we could not remain on the road. So the man had, for once, to find work to pay for a lodging. In return for help with the haying, a farmer gave us shelter and food for a little time. It was then I rode his carthorse, a poor, tired beast who could go no faster than a walk."

"May the saints preserve us!" Dickon said. "You should have told me."

"And have the two of you looking at me as if I were a bear upon your backs? Not I. Get on with it, Dickon. I shall manage." She hoped she sounded surer than she felt.

Dickon didn't argue with her. He turned his horse again and pricked him to a canter and rode ahead to where Robin, conscious the others were not upon his heels, had pulled up by the roadside to wait with what patience he could summon.

Cicely gathered her will and bade her knees obey her and managed to straighten in the saddle. The small respite had helped, but she knew it would not be long before the strain and the aches would come again. If Robin would only go a little slower, she could, maybe, do well enough. It was the insistent, the constant jogging that was the trouble.

Robin said, as Dickon joined him, "What was that about? Cicely having trouble with her stirrups?"

"Worse," Dickon answered. "She's not been on a horse for eight years and then on nothing but a farmer's nag, half-dead with age to hear her tell it. We'll have to slow our pace, Robin. She has courage enough and she's bound we'll not be stayed for her. But I tell you she'll never reach London *or* Windsor if we keep on as we've been going."

"Zounds!" Robin said, and did not trouble to hold his disgust in check. "This is what comes of having a girl in tow."

"She can't help it, Robin." Dickon rushed to her defense. "She wouldn't even admit discomfort till I pressed her."

Robin scowled but he said nothing for a minute, sitting with his head on one side and his forehead crinkled in a frown. Cicely came up before he spoke again and he was careful to keep any sound of censure from his voice. He could see by her face she was miserable and he had to credit her with courage. He said, "Can you hold out a little longer, Cicely, if we go more slowly?"

"I *told* Dickon I would manage," she said. "Don't stay for me."

Now why had she said that? A slower pace was the one thing she most wanted in the world right now. The devil take her pride.

Robin must not have heard her, for he went on speaking as if she had said nothing. "I've been thinking," he said, "and I've remembered a posting house not far from here. The host—I'd not thought of him for years—once lived in Canterbury. My father did him a favor once and he was grateful. He's an honest fellow and can be trusted. He will, I'm sure, for my father's sake, find us a room and hot water for soaking the soreness out of you. By tomorrow you'll feel a deal better. You'll see. It's the strain on unused muscles that's troubling you."

Dickon said, "Thanks, Robin," but Cicely only nodded, too tired to say another word—and too relieved that her ordeal was almost over for the day.

"Let's go on, then," Robin said and clucked to his horse holding him on a tight rein to an easy walk.

He kept the slow pace but even so, Cicely's discomfort was only a little less. Still, it was no longer necessary to keep all her mind and her will fixed upon the need to hang to her saddle in order not to be jolted off the horse's back. For the first time in this day which seemed to her endless, she could think back over its events and try to order them in her mind.

Her thinking brought her small comfort. She was, it was true, no longer a girl alone in the hostile world of the road. She was no longer fair game for any man who might penetrate her disguise. She would come more quickly to London and, if Robin held to his promise, she would find a haven with his mother if she couldn't make her own way. Meantime she would be fed and at least have a bed to sleep in this night. So much was gained. But when she considered the matter of Jackdaw and Sparrow, the picture in her mind was all dark.

To be fair it wasn't Jackdaw who troubled her. He was not, she was sure, one of the evil ones. Not in himself. But he was slow-witted and easily led. It was Sparrow who, his small eyes gleaming wickedly, had urged Jackdaw on to discover her disguise. It was Sparrow she feared. It was all very well for Dickon to dismiss him as a man of no moment. But she was sure he had guessed she was a maid. She was sure he meant her real harm, there in Oxford town. She was sure he meant to have her and she doubted he would give up his intent easily. What's more, she had seen his face when he had dragged Jackdaw off. There had been hatred for Dickon in it; hatred and malice, and she guessed, shame at having been overcome before her.

What if he had not, in fact, gone his way as Dickon said? What if he were dogging their footsteps now, this minute, waiting his chance to revenge himself upon Dickon, then come for her?

She thought she heard a rustling in the hedges that lined their way and looked around, expecting to see him, with or without Jackdaw, on the road behind them. But the byway into which Robin had turned was empty and she chided herself for foolishness. Still, she wondered, should she not tell Dickon her thoughts?

She looked ahead and saw Dickon and Robin talking, their heads stretched sideways, as their horses picked their own way along the road. Better not interrupt them. Besides, she was too tired to make the small effort needed to cover the distance that had opened between them. What was worse she had no notion how to make this great brute of an animal beneath her quicken its pace. She'd tell Dickon later, when they had settled in this posting house Robin had mentioned.

Neither Robin nor Dickon was thinking at that moment of Cicely. They were discussing their chances of finding Marlowe. "We've got to find him, Dickon," Robin said. His face was clouded with worry.

Dickon nodded. "I wish," he said, "I knew more about him; more about the places he might be keeping himself; who his companions might be. I wish you knew him, Robin, as Ned Alleyn does."

Robin shrugged. "There's been small chance for that, Dickon. Marlowe, so Ned says, seldom leaves London except when he goes to Canterbury to see his

mother or here and there upon the Queen's business
—if he still is about those matters."

"You never saw him when you were playing in London?"

Robin laughed. "Once," he said, "I saw him. In Canterbury. You must know, Dickon, I've never played in London. You don't come all in a moment to a London playhouse. I've been learning my craft these past two years. Besides, it's not likely Christopher Marlowe would notice a beginning actor like me. And it hasn't mattered in the least until now."

"Don't you *want* to know him?" Dickon asked. "I think I'd rather sit at his feet and listen to his talk than—than anything else I can dream of."

"Perhaps you will, when we find him. For me, that's of no importance. It's his plays I want to know. Every one of them. By heart. The man? The man may go what ways he will. Good, bad, atheist, true believer, brawler or peacekeeper—I don't really care so long as he gives us players such works as *Dr. Faustus* and *The Jew of Malta* to act in. Each of his plays, it seems to me, is better than his last. And, for my part, that's why we must find him and make him believe his danger and take thought for it."

Dickon shook his head. How could anyone separate a man from his works—ignore the one and cleave to the other? A man and his works were one. He started to put his thought into words but Robin forestalled him. "There's our posthouse," he said, and pointed ahead to a place where their winding lane rejoined the high road. Dickon followed the pointing and saw the roof of the inn and the stableyard at the side.

The yard was deserted when Robin jumped out of his saddle and opened his mouth to shout for a stable-boy to see to the horses. "Robin!" Dickon called urgently to stop him. He pointed to Cicely. The extra miles, even at the slow pace Robin had set, had used up the last of her strength and she was slumped over the saddle, her face white with exhaustion. "Go ahead and explain about us, Robin," Dickon went on. "The horses will stand a bit. But Cicely will need help in dismounting. Better not to have an audience of boys gaping and gossiping when I get her down."

Robin nodded. "Can you manage alone?" he asked.

"Yes," Dickon replied. He was already off his horse and had an arm about Cicely.

Robin hesitated and Dickon said, "Will you be off, Robin? The less waiting while you bespeak a chamber the better."

Robin went quickly toward the door of the posting house and Dickon turned to Cicely. "Come, sweet," he said to her as if she were a child. "It's over now. We'll have you inside and easy in a trice if you'll just help a little. Sit straighter, kitten. Just a little. There."

He lifted her foot out of the stirrup and moved around the horse to release the other foot. "Now," he said, "can you reach down a little—just a little—and get your arms about my neck? Good. Keep them tight now."

He lifted her, amazed that any grown creature

should be so light of weight, and set her on the
ground. He kept one arm about her supporting her
and began to cajole her into walking. She looked at
him and managed a small smile to encourage them
both.

"I'm—truly—sorry—Dickon," she said. "I—can—
make—it. I think." She straightened her aching back
and took his arm. Slowly, tottering a little because of
the trembling of her leg muscles, they started toward
the house. Halfway there she felt the quivering muscles firm a little and dropped his arm and said, "I can
stand alone, now, Dickon. See to the horses."

Dickon gave her a sharp look. Some color had come
into her face and, though there was still an exhausted
look to her, he thought she would do for a moment.
He shouted for the stableboy and, when the lad came
running, Dickon put his arm through Cicely's, trying
to appear as if they two were strollers while giving her
all the support he could.

Robin and a stout, red-cheeked, kindly-eyed woman
were waiting in the doorway of the house. The woman
took one look at Cicely and clucked her tongue and
called over her shoulder, "Joel! Joel, come quickly and
carry this child to the room that was our girls before
they married and left us."

"I can carry her," Dickon said. "She weighs no more
than a goose feather."

But Joel was there, almost as if he had sprung from
the very air about them. He was a huge man with a
gentle face. He paid no attention to Dickon's words

but lifted Cicely and started with her up the stairs.

"Put her upon the bed," his wife called after him. "I'll be along directly. You two," she turned to Robin and Dickon, "come with me. You can make yourselves useful carrying the hot water for me. Fie upon you! Dressing a sweet young maid in men's clothes and setting her upon a great brute of a horse. You might at least have chosen her a gentle, small palfrey to carry a lady without stretching her near in two."

"But, Mistress Rose," Robin began to explain.

"Don't you 'Mistress Rose' me, Robin Lang, that I dandled on my knees when you were not yet out of swaddling clothes. All alike, you are, you men! Feckless. Unthinking. Now, get to work, you and your friend."

She had led them into a kitchen that stretched across the whole back of the house. A fire burned at either end of the room in two enormous fireplaces. On a crane over each fire hung a great black kettle. Mistress Rose pointed to a stack of leathern buckets in a corner. "Fill four of those with water from the kettles," she ordered, "and bring them to the room at the top of the stairs. And be sure to knock and not come blundering in without my leave, for I'll be making the young lady comfortable. When you're done you can just refill the kettles and *then* Joel will find you a sleeping place. You're lucky you came so early in the day else you'd likely find yourselves bedding down wherever you could find space on the floor! I tell you we're like to be fair crowded every day before nightfall at this season of the year."

She was gone back along the corridor before she had finished her sentence. Dickon said, "Whew! She is a tartar!"

"Not really," Robin said. "Her scolding covers as kind a heart as you'd find in all England. I'd forgotten what a good soul she is, for it's been a long, long time since I was in swaddling clothes! I don't doubt she'll have Cicely comfortable and healing before the evening comes. But a pox on the girl, Dickon, for not telling us she was no horsewoman. She's likely lost us half a day."

"I doubt we gave her much chance to tell us anything, Robin," Dickon said. "And I doubt anyone who had never ridden more than a farmer's plug for a few minutes in a farmyard could have guessed how soon she'd tire and the aching begin, once she was embarked upon a real ride. For me—I'd forgotten long since what could happen and I'll warrant you had, too. Anyway, what's done is done and there's no sense wasting time bemoaning it. Did you tell Mistress Rose and her goodman all Cicely's story?"

"No," Robin answered, "only so much as they needed to know. Are you done?"

They had been filling the buckets as they talked. Now, when Dickon had added one more ladle of steaming water to his load, they lifted them and went up to the room at the top of the stairs. As Dickon raised his hand to knock, the door flew open and Mistress Rose, face tight with anger, began to shout, "Where in Tophet is. . . ? Oh! There you are and high time, too. Here, do you pass me those buckets. No. You are not to come in. My little lady's in no fit state for visitors." She took the last bucket into the room and slammed the door in their faces, leaving them standing in the dim hall like a pair of dummies.

Dickon turned restlessly in the bed he shared with Robin in a chamber under the eaves of the posting house. It must be past midnight. His body ached with tiredness after the long day. The little cut on his shoulder hurt and he could find no way to ease it. He longed for sleep as an unsuccessful beggar longs for food, but sleep would not come.

Glory, it was hot! Why did people have to sleep in dark caves, made airless by ells of heavy cloth closing the bedstead right in upon the sleeper? Could he, without waking Robin, push the draperies aside and watch the moon, playing blind-man's-buff with clouds, throw changing shadows about the bare, scrubbed floors? Better not chance it.

Something was, between one breath and the next, different in the room. What was it. Some sound? He listened. No. The room was quiet enough except for the ordinary creakings and rustlings a house made at night, as if it talked to itself, once its human occupants were in bed. Nor was there any change in the light. The cave of the bed was as dark as ever. Robin, too, was the same, flung upon his back, not moving beyond the orderly coming and going of his breath.

And yet there was something. Some difference. He had it now! There was a difference in the feel of the air. Even inside here it seemed fresher, less heavy, as if someone had opened the many-paned window and let in the night. If someone had stolen into the room by the window to take his jewel. . . .

It would be easy enough to do. Climb the twisted rope of the ivy stem outside, push the casement open, and there you were. He'd even noticed when Joel had brought them here, the casement had lost its fastening.

Even while these thoughts ran in his mind he had been gathering himself to push through the curtains and surprise the intruder. He moved slowly, with great care. He had tried to waken Robin but Robin was a sound sleeper and there was no time to shake him long enough to rouse him. No matter. He would do well enough alone. He would surprise the thief who would likely not expect to find anyone awake, and grab him, and take him to Joel who would hold him till a constable could be summoned from the nearest town.

His groping hand found the bed curtain and started to part it. Cautiously he made a crack no wider than the fraction of an inch, set his eyes to it, and met the eye of the person on the other side. The man's arm and hand were already reaching out toward the curtains. For one heartbeat both were held as if a witch-spell had been laid on them. Then the intruder cursed softly and Dickon lunged into the room. As he did so, his feet tangled with the folds of the curtain and he fell sprawling. He was up in an instant and, as he came erect, recognized Sparrow for the moon was, now, making a radiance in the room. Sparrow was at the window tugging at the casement which had somehow swung shut in such a way as to wedge itself tight.

"You!" Dickon said. "What are you doing here? Did you come creeping to take me unaware and finish the job of killing me you failed to complete this morning?"

He went after Sparrow, but the small mishap with the curtains had lost enough time and Sparrow wrenched open the window and threw himself head-long through it while Dickon was still not halfway across the room. He leaned from the casement, when he reached it, but the inconstant moon was once more cloud-shrouded and, when the shadow had passed, there was no sign of Sparrow. Dickon wondered if he should rouse the household and decided not to. By the time he could get them up and explain and start a search, Sparrow would be safely hidden. He was sure of that.

He pulled forward a chair with a tall, heavy back and rammed it against the window. Not that he ex-pected Sparrow to come again. Still, better be safe. He went back across the room and sat on the bedstead, rubbing his shoulder to relieve its aching. Had Sparrow come to kill him or had he in some manner found out about the jewel and come after it? Or both?

He spoke over his shoulder to Robin. "And where were you, brave Robin, in all this?"

There was no answer. Dickon pulled the drapery aside and looked at the bed and couldn't believe Robin was still asleep.

Dickon sighed, wishing he could sleep as soundly. An army with banners passing through the room would likely not wake Robin. Nor, from the silence in the house, had anyone else been roused. Leaving the curtains parted, he lay on the bed and closed his eyes once more, preparing to wait out the night in wakefulness. Almost immediately, the sleep he had so long courted came to him and blanked out all his scurrying thoughts.

CHAPTER X
Threat

The sun, now reaching its early morning warmth through the opened bed curtains, waked Dickon and Robin not long after its rising. They lay, lazily, side by side for a few minutes, not talking, adjusting their minds to the strange room and the new day, still half held in the cocoon of sleep.

Robin spoke first. "Another day of sun. We're fortunate in the weather at least. Zounds! the bed curtains are open. Now how in. . . ."

Dickon was, suddenly, wide awake and aware of all that had happened during the night. He jerked straight up in the bed and glared at Robin. "And, sweet Robin," he said, "what a chance *you* missed. If you'd slept less soundly we might have caught a thief —or worse."

"Wha—what are you saying, Dickon Fontayne?" Robin asked when he could get his mouth closed over his astonishment.

"The truth, Robin. That Sparrow I told you of came in the night. Climbed up the ivy tree and through the window that's lost its catch. I'd have caught him, too, except for my clumsy feet which tripped me and I lost a minute untangling myself. By the time I could be after him he'd got himself clear of the room. And even the moon helped him for it hid behind clouds until he could lose himself."

"Why didn't you wake me, Dickon?"

"Easier to wake the dead. When you sleep, you *sleep*! There was no time to shake you awake if I was to go after him. If it hadn't been for those misbegotten bedclothes. . . ."

"Did you wake Joel? Did he find the villain?"

"There was no reason to. No harm had come to us. There'd not been time for Sparrow to seize the jewel —if that was what he came for. I suspect he wanted to kill me in revenge for the small beating he took from me. But if that was his reason he failed, for here I am hale and whole. And it was plain the thief could have lost himself in a thousand safe hiding places before I could ever have roused the house. No, Joel doesn't know of this."

"Then we'd better tell him; warn him," Robin said.

"No, Robin. Think. It's clear enough this Sparrow was after *me*. If he'd been an ordinary thief come to rob quickly and easily as he might, he would not, surely, have chosen the highest window in the house. He must have been lurking about and spying upon us so he could be sure where we would sleep. He failed in his ends with me and it follows, then, especially as he was nearly caught, he will not come back here. But we'd likely be wise to keep our eyes sharp till we get to London. He might follow us again as he must have done when we left Oxford, though I saw no sign of him upon the road. Besides, if we mention this to Joel he'll be in such a pother we'll likely lose another day. And that we'd better not risk if we are, in truth, working against time to warn Christopher Marlowe. I wish I could be sure of that."

Robin nodded. "You're right, Dickon. For a little I'd forgotten why we were going to London. But I will remind Joel to mend the catch on that window. So much we owe to his kindness and Mistress Rose's, for likely enough that latch has just slipped his mind."

Dickon went to the door and opened it and listened. "The house is stirring," he said. "Now if Cicely's only awake and able to ride we can move out upon the road and get a start before it's clogged with people."

He moved the chair from its protective place before the window while Robin dashed cold water from the ewer upon his face and hands and dried them on the rough linen towel by the washhand stand. When Dickon had done the same, they dressed themselves and shouldered their luggage and started down the stairs.

Dickon fingered the jewel about his neck, checking its safety. He must be extra careful of it from now on. And of his tongue—that he would not give away the presence of his only wealth.

"Will we be able to find an easier mount for Cicely, Robin? Mistress Rose is right. That great gelding has much too broad a back for her short legs."

"I doubt Mistress Rose would hear of our starting out otherwise," Robin laughed. "For ourselves I'd reckon the horses we came on will do well enough. They are good mounts and, by the gods, we tired them not at all yesterday! Now stop looking like a summer storm, Dickon. A body'd think you were besotted over that girl the way you jump to anger if you so much as imagine a slight to her highness."

Dickon, behind Robin, stopped with one foot on the step below him. Besotted over Cicely! Robin had lost his wits. Or had he? Was Dickon Fontayne indeed in danger of losing his head and his heart over a creature of the road with pretensions to a grand birthright?

Robin said, "Dickon! What's got into you? You've the look of a lost cow mooning there on the steps."

Dickon shook himself and continued his way down the stairs. He gave Robin no answer. He was not going to tell him all his thoughts. But Robin was not willing to let it alone.

"What has got into you, Dickon?" he said again.

"Nothing!" Dickon almost spat the word at him. "Let me be, Robin. My thoughts are my own and don't forget it."

"Say you so?" Robin sounded both irritated and, a little, hurt by his brusqueness. "You've no cause to be rude, Dickon."

"I'm sorry," Dickon said and knew he spoke no more

than the truth. He should not have flown in anger at
Robin. He put his hand on Robin's shoulder. "Let's
not quarrel, Robin," he said. "It was truly nothing but
a vagrant thought, already forgotten. I slept little last
night and it's made me testy."

Robin was not one to hold a grudge for long. He
smiled at Dickon. "It's forgotten," he said. "And there's
our Cicely above you, looking cool as you please and
ready to ride, or my eyes are deceitful wretches. Are
you feeling better, girl?"

"That I am," Cicely said and ran down the steps to
join them. "Only I'm hungry as—as the lion in the
Queen's menagerie at the Tower."

"Come along then," Dickon said, holding out his
hand to her. "We'll break our fast and see what Goodman Joel has in his stables fit for a lass to ride."

They rode away from the posting house an hour
later, full of advice from Mistress Rose. Joel had himself brought around a beautiful little mare for Cicely.
The saddle was carefully padded but the padding was
cleverly concealed so the casual eye would notice nothing. "Leave the horses with my friend Simon Smith in
Deptford," Joel told them. "He'll see the mare and saddle come home to me in time." He started to help
Cicely into the saddle but she waved him off and, after
one unsuccessful try, got herself mounted and waited,
feeling triumphant, while Joel adjusted the stirrups.
Satisfied that she was securely seated, he waved them
on their way, refusing to take a farthing for their
night's entertainment.

The day was fresh and the road nearly empty. In spite of their serious errand, their spirits were high. Cicely was gayest of the three, breaking now and then into snatches of song in a remarkably sweet voice. She rode comfortably upon the smaller horse, almost as easily as Robin and Dickon. She learns fast, Dickon thought, and felt pride in her.

They had told her about Sparrow's visit the night before, as soon as they were out of earshot of the posting house, and warned her to keep her eyes and ears open for any sign of the little man or his friend Jackdaw. She had shivered a little at the tale and frowned, but she said only, "Was Jackdaw there too, then, Dickon?"

"I didn't see him," Dickon answered. "But it would follow, I'd think, that where Sparrow is there you'll find Jackdaw as well. He was, likely, keeping watch below or some such thing."

"Likely," she said aloud but she wondered. She could not think Jackdaw would take any part in such a venture.

"We'd better go single file," Robin said, "with Cicely between us. That way she'll be safer. I'll lead for I know the road well. You come behind, Dickon, and guard our backs."

"And let us know if the pace is too fast for you or if you tire, Cicely," Dickon warned her as they made their line.

But Cicely didn't seem the same girl who had drooped so easily yesterday. Mistress Rose, knowing just what to do, had managed to mend her aches completely. Cicely could still feel the comfort of hot water smelling of some piney stuff. She felt no more than a little stiffness, which was already passing.

Dickon, watching her, thought she'd do. She was getting the feel of riding. She had, indeed, the makings of a fine horsewoman, sitting straight in the saddle, and guiding the mare with firm but gentle hands as if she'd been born to it. He should, he knew, be examining Robin's charge that he was besotted over her. But the day was too fine for problems, beyond the chief one of finding Marlowe and warning him of his danger. And, for this moment, they were doing all they could about that. He'd put off probing his feelings about Cicely until they had finished their quest.

They stopped for a meal at Windsor and, when they had finished and gone into the street they saw above them the royal castle. Dickon said, "Let's go closer the better to see it."

Robin's unadorned "No" was quick and positive.

"But why not?" Cicely put in before Dickon could protest. She'd like a closer look herself.

Robin glanced at her as if she had been a grub-worm, lacking all sense, and did not answer.

"Look, Robin," Dickon said, "it wouldn't take all that much time just to go close enough to see it properly. We could at least watch the changing of the Queen's Guard." He was pleading now. Tom had been here once and had brought home tales of the splendors within. There was, Tom had said, an unbelievable bustle of comings and goings, of color and sound. Dickon wanted to look for himself. In some way it seemed to him that looking would bring Tom back for a moment.

But Robin wouldn't listen. "We'll come back, Dickon," he said. "We mustn't take the time now. If we're lucky and push on steadily we can be in London tonight. But not if we stop to see all the sights along the way."

Time, time, time, Cicely thought. She was sick of the sound of the word, for whenever Robin spoke it he seemed to be accusing her. What did it matter whether they came to London tonight or tomorrow? An hour lost while Dickon had his look at the Queen's castle would do no harm. Why didn't he argue with Robin, *make* him wait? After all this was Dickon's business in the first place, fool's errand that it was in her opinion. Dickon was too gentle by far.

Gentle! She had to laugh at herself remembering this "gentle" Dickon laying the giant Jackdaw flat with one good blow before he turned on the man with the dagger and cooked his goose for him. The inner laughter drove away her irritation and, as they rode out of town on the road to London she was, once more, humming to herself—but softly for the way was anthill-busy now with travelers.

Dickon looked back over his shoulder at the town nestling close beneath the walls and towers of gray stone. The castle seemed to hang suspended between earth and air, outlined against blue sky. The Queen's flag, showing she was in residence, lifted in an idle breeze and hung slack once more upon its staff. How he wished he could have gone about the public parts of Windsor Castle. Maybe they would have caught sight of Gloriana herself. Likely she was here to get away from the plague. He'd heard it said somewhere that Windsor was her favorite residence. And no wonder. For in spite of the curtain wall that rose steep and straight for many feet above the ditch at its base, in spite of the dark battlements designed to protect the monarch from enemy attack in olden days when wars were fought with lance and spear, bow and arrow, and cauldrons of boiling pitch rather than with gunpowder, the fortress-castle had a graciousness, a peaceful feeling, that made you forget it had been made for war.

But Robin was right, of course. Each hour, each minute counted if they were to warn Christopher Marlowe in time.

But he wished Robin had not taken over the venture. Likely Robin was more used to making decisions, to ordering people about. Certainly it was easier to go quickly with horses and with someone who knew every road in England, it seemed, as he knew the back of his hand. But it would be more comfortable to the spirit of Dickon Fontayne if he had something to say about their actions. Well, that was how it was. Marlowe himself had written the line *"Che sera, sera,"* what will be,

will be. As well turn his mind away from disappointment and enjoy the day.

The road was crowded with the usual flotsam of
human dregs. Only, here, the people who lived on the
road and by it were, more often than not, jostled aside
by luckier folk on horseback or in carriages that rum-
bled with bone-breaking jerks over the rutted surface,
followed by the curses of the walkers forced out of the
way. Better ruts than mud. How long would the sun
shine? He couldn't remember so rainless a spring.
Hard on the growing things but. . . .

"Hist!"

The sharp sibilant penetrated his musing and
brought him to the guilty realization he'd forgotten to
keep a lookout for their enemies. The sound came
from ahead and, looking toward it, he saw Cicely half
turned in her saddle beckoning to him. He urged his
horse over the few feet between them.

"What is it?" he asked and added a caution. "Mind
you speak softly."

"I thought I saw Jackdaw," Cicely said so quietly he
had to strain to catch the words.

"Where?"

"Behind the thorn hedge, half a dozen paces back.
Watching us."

"Are you sure?"

"No. But nearly so. *Somebody* was there."

"Come."

They rode side by side until they were abreast of
Robin.

"Cicely thinks she just saw Jackdaw watching us," Dickon said and waited for Robin to tell them what to do.

Robin pinched his lip and stared ahead and said nothing. Was it possible he didn't know what course to take?

"So, what shall we do, Robin?" Dickon insisted. This was no time for clogging the road while Robin thought.

"I—don't—know, Dickon," Robin said and fidgeted, ashamed he couldn't give Dickon a quick answer.

Dickon stared at him for a second. In all the time he'd known Robin he'd never seen him at a loss for an answer. "But—but, Robin," he began.

"See here, Dickon," Robin said. He was blustering a little, no doubt to hide his embarrassment. "I know no more than you what we should do. I'm more accustomed to make-believe problems than to real ones. Actors. . . ."

"You were quick enough with plans and schemes for dressing Cicely and thinking of a place to stay last night."

"That! We're all accustomed to such things when we travel the roads with our plays. But this. . . ."

"Never mind," Dickon cut in. So, now it was up to him. He'd have to decide how to handle this situation. He'd got his wish right enough. First thing was to get off the road.

He looked about him and saw a copse of beech trees in a fallow field bordering the road. He touched his horse and guided it through a gap in the thorn hedge. Cicely was beside him in a minute and, after another minute, he heard Robin clopping behind.

Not one of them spoke. Dickon thought he would best consider the various plans of action open to them as if he were considering a problem in logic at Cambridge. He set his mind to examine each alternative in turn.

They could return to the road and ride on, pretending they hadn't seen Jackdaw, and trust the crowds to protect them from attack. But they'd hardly reach London before dark and by that time the road would, very likely, be deserted, or nearly so. That might be just what their enemies hoped they would do. They'd be tired and alone and easy to attack. He and Robin could, doubtless, protect themselves well enough, though he still didn't know what Robin could do in a real fight. But there was Cicely. And if they were set upon without warning, Cicely might be harmed. He'd not chance that.

Then suppose they turned back to Windsor and went to the constable and said they were afraid of being set upon. Would the constable believe them? Especially if he saw through Cicely's disguise as Robin had done so easily. He might, suspicious of a masquerading girl, throw them into jail. And even if he did believe them, could he hold Jackdaw and, likely, Sparrow upon suspicion only? Furthermore, such a course would delay them, no man could tell how long.

Then there was nothing to do but go to meet trouble. He sighed a little. At least they would be prepared for it. They could force the fight, if it came to that, on their own ground.

Rapidly, he outlined his thinking for Robin and Cicely. Cicely nodded agreement to each point he made. Robin, looking hangdog, gave no sign until Dickon said, "Well, Robin?"

"Agreed," Robin said shortly.

"It may come to a fight, Robin. Can you—are you with me?"

Robin smiled faintly. "You can count on me in a fight, Dickon," he said. "That I can do off stage as well as on. An actor's life is none so peaceful he can afford to be defenseless. That was one of the first things Ned Alleyn taught me. A mob of yokels, if they don't like your play, aren't slow to vent their anger upon your body. Oh yes, I can fight if it comes to that."

Dickon felt his breath actually come more easily from his chest. If Robin could make a good fight, their problem was no problem at all. The big man would give little trouble and together they could handle Sparrow, dagger and all. "Now," he said, "just where did you see Jackdaw, Cicely, exactly."

She turned and pointed to the row of thorn bushes that lined the road. Their white blossoms, catching the early afternoon sun and reflecting it, made a line of light and beauty, but none of the three saw it. Their eyes were turned inward as they concentrated upon their need. "One, two, three, four, five," Cicely counted aloud as she ran her eyes along each bush. "It was there, behind the fifth bush, I saw him."

"You're sure, Cicely?"

"Sure of the bush. Very nearly sure it was Jacksaw."

"Then we'll search for him—and Sparrow—there or thereabouts," Dickon said. "On foot," he added and dismounted.

The others joined him on the ground and Robin said, showing some enthusiasm for the first time since he'd acknowledged his lack of ability to advise them in this emergency, "Let's get on with it then," and started walking toward the hedge with Cicely close behind him.

"Wait!" Dickon ordered.

They stopped and looked at him, questioning. For a moment he knew a feeling of triumph. They had so readily accepted him as their leader—he, Dickon Fontayne, the scholar, the dreamer, never before the man of action. This had not happened to him before and his pride took stature from it. He wished he had more time to savor the new pleasure; wished Tom could see him now. But there was no time.

"Not you, Cicely," he said.

"But, Dickon. . . ."

"Don't argue, girl, and think. You'd be no possible help in a fight and would only put yourself—and us —in danger."

"And would I not be a help?" she said. Dickon was amused to see she was angry. "Never gainsay a lady's ability to fight, Dickon Fontayne. Can I not bite and scratch as well as the next?"

"And likely get Sparrow's dagger in your ribs for your pains. That one wouldn't, I'd vow, care that you're a girl. No, Cicely, you will do us the greater service if you stay here with the horses. Then, should our enemies get the best of us, you're to ride straightaway to London and find Mistress Alleyn and give her this." He fumbled the letter from his purse and handed it to her. "And you're to tell Mistress Alleyn all you've heard us say of Master Christopher Marlowe and tell her to warn him of his danger."

Cicely looked her rebellion for a heartbeat more. Then, without more comment, she turned and gathered the reins of the horses and started toward the trees.

CHAPTER XI

Warning!

"Now!" Dickon said and began to move stealthily toward the thorn hedge. He went one cautious step and whirled again as a voice said, "Young Master."

"Who speaks?" Dickon asked. The skin seemed to creep along the back of his neck at words that might have come out of nowhere.

"Jackdaw."

"Where are you, villain? Come out and let me get my hands on you and your friend Sparrow."

"Now, young sir, Sparrow's no friend of mine unless you'd call a chance companion of the road friend. But it's no matter for he's not here. We parted company when he went to steal your jewel for vengeance because you bested him in the fight at Oxford town."

Dickon, searching all the space about him trying to find Jackdaw, said, "A pox on you. Come where I can see you, if you dare."

"That I do not," said the disembodied voice mildly.

"For you and your friend would batter me to pieces before I could get my mouth open. Not that I'm much of a fighter, as you well know. No, young sir, I'll not show myself. Not yet. But I've a thing to tell you—a thing you should know, and I'll not tell it or let you see me till you've promised me safety."

"And that I'll not do," Dickon said. "Why should I promise you anything but a good beating? Weren't you threatening my young friend when last I saw you. Didn't I warn you to leave us alone if you wanted to stay hale?"

"Now, young sir. I meant the lass no harm and would have told you so, had you given me the chance. I was only having a bit of fun with her, dressed up like a draggled popinjay, pretending to be a man."

"So you say. But I don't believe you. So keep your thoughts to yourself. I doubt I need anything you can tell me. Come, friends, we'll be off."

He reached to take the reins from Cicely but she held them so tightly he couldn't wrench them from her without hurting her. "Don't be a fool, Dickon," she said. He put his finger to his lips, cautioning her and she laughed. "Would you lock the stable door after the horse is gone? The masquerade is over with Jackdaw. Listen to the man, Dickon. Or are you afraid of him—you and Robin?"

There was scorn in her voice and it flicked at Dickon's new-found pride.

"You think I fear him?" he asked.

"If you don't why won't you give him the promise he asks and hear him out?"

She spoke truly. He wasn't thinking clearly. He took another minute to set his mind to rights and said, "Very well then, Jackdaw. We'll listen. You may come out from wherever you're hiding without fear of us."

There was a slight movement among the leaves above their heads and Jackdaw was beside Dickon before he could take a breath. For all his size Jackdaw had landed as lightly as a falling leaf.

"So, here I am, young sir," he said. "Why don't we sit beneath the trees for our talk, for to say true I had little sleep last night and am weary."

Dickon was looking all about him again, more than half expecting Sparrow to leap at them in spite of the big man's assurance he was alone. But he could see nothing suspicious and he began to relax his caution and listen.

The others had already seated themselves on the soft leaf mold that made a cushion on the ground. As Dickon joined them he said, "Do stop calling me 'young sir,' Jackdaw. My name is Dickon Fontayne."

"That I will then, Master Dickon," Jackdaw said and grinned at him in friendliness.

Dickon said, "Now what is all this, Jackdaw?"

"I thought to warn you, Master Dickon. I know you foiled Sparrow in some way about the jewel. But I doubt you're safe as yet."

"How did you know about the jewel?" Dickon's suspicions flared again. Was this some trick after all—a trick to give Sparrow time to get into position to way-lay them?

Jackdaw made a gesture as if he would say that was of no moment. "We quarreled about it, for I would have no part in his plan to steal it. He told me to be off then and called me names, and I went a little away from him as if I were going back to Oxford. But I didn't go far. I hid myself and waited and watched. He stood as if he were thinking, then went into a pasture and slept awhile. When he woke he stood about for a bit, first on one foot, then on t' other, for all the world as if he were a great awkward bird making up its mind to fly. All this was at the place where you paused when the lass could no longer ride easily. We'd followed you, you see, going by short ways, from Oxford where Sparrow had seen your jewel at The Bull."

He paused as if for a comment. When no one spoke he went on.

"Then, when he'd done his thinking, Sparrow gave himself a great shake and nodded his head twice or thrice and took to the road again, and I followed him at a safe distance. He waited till dark near your posting house, listening at windows and spying out the land. I would have grappled him when he started for the ivy tree. But he's a sly one and too quick for me. I didn't see him again until he came tumbling down and mumbling to himself and cursing 'the devil's spawn' which is the way he calls you for a 'wakeful brat.' And I knew, then, he had no jewel."

"But why? Why did you follow him?"

"Because, Master Dickon, I don't like the little man."

"Don't—don't like him?" Robin said. "But you were his companion. You walked the road with him."

Jackdaw looked his confusion. He struggled to find words that would explain what he didn't wholly understand himself. How could he make these fine young gentlemen comprehend the ways of the road?

Cicely came to his rescue. "Be quiet, Robin," she ordered. "You and all your fine company of players know little of the real road. It makes strange bedfellows and no man can say why he takes this one or that for companion. You're lonely and there's someone for keeping you company. Or you're weak and another's strong. Or you've a fancy to share a meal. Or a thousand other reasons. It doesn't matter."

"Thank you, lass," Jackdaw said.

"But why did you come after us? And how did you know where to find us? And how did you come here before us since we are mounted and you're afoot?" The questions tumbled from Dickon.

Jackdaw raised his hand, palm out, as if he would hold back the spate of words. "Softly, Master Dickon," he said. "Please to remember I'm not overly quick-witted."

"I'm sorry," Dickon muttered.

"Now for your questions. It was none so hard to know you'd pass this way, for did you not declare in Oxford you were bound for London? Nor did I come

on foot. When Sparrow had left the posting house I
went to my ho . . . , to a place I know of and slept
awhile. But I was up before the first gray light began
in the east and borrowed a horse. It's waiting for me
now in Windsor. I came here and hid myself on the
London road and waited for you. As to why I came. I
came to warn you as I said just now."

Dickon pulled his long legs under him and stood
up. He couldn't think sitting on the cushiony earth
and he wanted his mind as clear as possible. Though
he must own to a growing liking for this simple-simon
of a man, he could not rid himself of a notion that all
this was a trick; that at any moment Sparrow would
come from some hiding place and attack them, thinking them lulled to a feeling of safety by Jackdaw's talk.
Why should Jackdaw go to so much trouble to warn
them?

He walked all the way around the little stand of
trees but he saw no one, no sign of danger. He came
back to look down at Jackdaw, sprawled at his ease
upon the leaf mold, a twig between his teeth like any
country bumpkin.

Dickon put his question into words. "Why? Why do
you think I need warning, Jackdaw?"

Jackdaw removed the twig and spat out its juices before he answered. "Because, Master Dickon, Sparrow
wants three things from you, as he was at pains to tell
me while we stalked you as if you were wild deer. He
wants revenge because you wouldn't let him kill you

there in Oxford. He wants the jewel you carry. And he wants the lady who's under your protection."

"But," Dickon said and stopped when Jackdaw held up his hand.

"Hear me out, Master Dickon, so you'll know the whole about this Sparrow. The little man's not what he seems to be. I have no doubt you'll take care enough upon the road to London, since you've had a taste of his ways. But Sparrow's no ordinary knight of the road but a far more dangerous kind of person. He'll be after you right enough on his own grounds in London, which is where he belongs. So you should know you've likely not seen the last of him."

"How do you know all this, Jackdaw?" Cicely put in. "Few road people will talk of themselves."

"Sparrow had a deal too much wine one night, Mistress, and could not forbear boasting of himself and his friends. He belongs to London where he's known, he said, as a sharp one. He wouldn't say what he was doing on the road. But I've a notion he was in some trouble in London and had taken to wandering till the hue and cry abated. This I do know. He had money in plenty in his pocket. I first saw him six months ago and it's reasonable enough he should feel safe to go to his home now, and that's what he's doing. I'll wager my life on it."

Dickon pulled at his ear, thinking. He was not so much afraid of Sparrow. He himself wouldn't likely, be long in London and, now he was forewarned, he thought he could give a good enough account of himself should an attack come. But he was nagged by the feeling that all this somehow tied in with the plot against Marlowe. Thinking back upon the fight in Oxford, he was sure Sparrow had spoken Marlowe's name and spoken it with scorn and familiarity. If he could find out more about Sparrow's associates he might, perhaps, have names to bring to Marlowe and so give his warning more weight. He'd heard Tom say London's thieves and rascals stuck together. If he could discover who some of them were. . . .

"What about these friends you heard him boast of?" he asked Jackdaw. "What do they do in London?"

"Little more than think up ways to fleece their neighbors, to hear Sparrow talk." A slow grin began at the corners of Jackdaw's mouth and spread to his eyes. It transformed his sad face until he looked like a great friendly beast asking for a pat on the head. "His particular friend, one Frizer. . . ."

"Frizer?" Dickon asked. The name ran in his head like a warning bell, but warning him of what he couldn't tell. He was sure he'd heard it before, but for his life he couldn't remember where at this moment. "Frizer? Frizer what?"

"Indeed I don't know for Sparrow only spoke the single name in my hearing. But this Frizer pretended to steal the old guns on Tower Hill and sell them to a credulous young gentleman. Frizer so confused the gull, he was the wealthier by upwards of sixty pounds *and* the guns, you'll understand, still safe in their places by the Tower."

He stopped to chuckle over his story. Cicely made an admiring sound and Robin said, "By my faith! The gull deserved what he got, I'm thinking."

Dickon ignored them. Frizer, Frizer, Frizer. He wished he could remember. But at least here was one name to mark, maybe to find out more about when they came to Mistress Alleyn. Were there other names?

"Did Sparrow name others in his talk?" he asked Jackdaw.

"None I recall. No! Wait! He did speak two other names, spoke them with respect and boasting, as if knowing them somehow set Sparrow apart. Skeres. And Poley."

"Robert Poley?" Robin asked quickly.

Jackdaw shrugged. "He said no more than Poley."

"Why, Robin?" Dickon asked. "Does that name mean something special to you? Something connected with Christopher Marlowe?"

Robin didn't answer at once. "I wonder now," he said to himself. "I do wonder."

"What, Robin?" Dickon said. "What's in your mind?"

"Take Robert Poley now," Robin said. "He's well known for a scoundrel. Alleyn knows him and says he's not to be trusted an inch. He's one of the worst types of men Walsingham used upon the Queen's business, though Sir Francis, when he was alive, so Alleyn said, did not trust him far. He was busy in the matter of the Queen of Scots and helped bring about her execution by laying bare the plot to free her from her prison at Fotheringay Castle. And he did so by betraying a close friend. For a price. He's been in all the Queen's prisons, though whether to spy upon other prisoners or for crimes of his own doing I cannot say. And—here's the rub, Dickon—he's close to Kit Marlowe. If he should fear something hidden in Marlowe's mind, or if he should be in the pay of someone else who fears. . . . But this may not be the same Poley Sparrow spoke of, of course."

"Did Sparrow ever speak of one Christopher Marlowe, the poet and playmaker?" Dickon asked Jackdaw who had been listening to all they were saying without understanding much of what it was about. He answered quickly, now, and with assurance.

"No, Master Dickon. And that's a name I'd surely remember for I've stood outside many an innyard and listened to some company of players speaking his words—and fine words they were to boot."

Dickon pulled at his ear again. Was there any other information he could get from Jackdaw he wondered. "Do you know where any of these men live in London?" he asked at last.

"That I do not. I doubt Sparrow knows himself, for I'd warrant he moves from one hole to another, keeping ahead of the constables. Besides, it isn't likely any of them's in London now, for all who can have fled the place because of the plague. I remember Sparrow did say, and proudly, both Frizer and Poley were often abroad. And he mentioned that Frizer is Thomas Walsingham's man—or his lady's."

"*Thomas* Walsingham?" Cicely put in. "I thought his name was Francis."

"Sir Francis' cousin, this Thomas," Robin explained. "He's known to be hand and glove with many a strange character. I've heard it said he's busy spying on the Catholics in Kent. Yes, and, by Harry! Our Kit's his man as well."

Dickon shook his head. He remembered where he'd heard the name Frizer. Tom had spoken it. Could this Frizer, then, and this Poley be the men whose talk Tom had overheard? Did this tangle of names, these hints at deep, unnamed wickedness have, in truth, then, a bearing on their quest? How many men named Frizer were there in England? Did the name mean anything? He wished he could find one single loose strand in the tangle to tug and so unravel the whole. Jackdaw was speaking again. He'd best listen.

". . . caution you again about Sparrow. Likely he'll be the angrier because he lost your jewel. He's bent on vengeance, remember, and he knows you're going to London. What's more he knows you'll seek out Mistress Alleyn."

"How?" Dickon asked. "How could he possibly know that?"

"He was at The Bull at Oxford, as I told you. He

said he was near enough to touch you and you none
the wiser. He overheard all your talk."

Cicely said, "Take the lesson to heart, Dickon. In future, be careful what you say in public places."

Jackdaw nodded. "And have a care for yourselves—
all of you and especially the lass—that Sparrow doesn't
creep upon your backs with murder in his black
heart."

Robin said, "Is there nothing else you can tell us?"

"No. Sparrow kept a close mouth when he was not
drinking and that was most of the time. I doubt he
knew how much he'd said of himself and his friends, or
thought I was too dull-witted to read his words
aright."

Dickon said, "Thank you, Jackdaw. We all thank
you for the trouble you've taken for our sakes. And
we'll be careful. It won't be so easy for Sparrow to take
us unawares now."

He paused to swallow hard before he went on. "And
I—I beg your pardon for—for mistaking your aim at
Oxford. I am, in all truth, sorry I knocked you down
without waiting to hear you out. If I can make
amends. . . ."

"Don't distress yourself, Master Dickon. Overhasty
you were and I must say it, but who could blame you
when you thought I was bent upon molesting your
lady. And indeed you're wise to hide her in men's
clothes, for the road's full of scoundrels who'd as soon
dishonor a maid as look at her. But it was a good turn
you did me for, as I lay upon my back in the dust, it

came to me I'd had enough of the road. From now on I shall have a new life to live."

"But—but, what will you do?" Cicely asked. "It's not so easy to make your way in these times if you've had no place but the road."

Jackdaw hesitated. The habits of years spent in keeping his own counsel, of fearing the motives of anyone who asked questions, were hard to break. But there was, in truth, no reason why he should keep silent now. Not any longer.

"I'll do well enough, lass," he said, and smiled at her. "I have only to swallow my pride and go home to my parents, back to helping with the farming as I used to do. My father was so angered when he found I was not quick-witted enough for the parson he wanted me to be, he ranted and raved at me as if I were a very villain. His anger sparked mine and I left his hearth. He has a farm near Oxford and it was there I spent a part of last night, though he doesn't know it yet. I spoke to my mother and she says he's old now and needs my help. He'll welcome me back for the price of a pardon asked and granted."

He got to his feet and stood looking at her. "I'm sorry I thought to make a mock of you, lass," he said. "It was an evil thing to do. But I meant you no real harm and I'll take my oath to that."

Cicely, in her turn, got up from the carpet of leaf mold. She put her hand gently upon his arm. "I know it now, Jackdaw," she said. "I was stupid then and afraid."

"My name's John Howland, lass," he said. "I'm leaving Jackdaw behind—on the road." He touched her cropped hair gently and turned to leave them.

Cicely said, with urgency, stopping him, "John Howland, wait!"

He stopped and looked back at her and she asked, "Did—did you know the man and woman who called me their daughter? Really know them?"

Jackdaw's eyes grew almost black with some emotion Cicely could not name. But his voice was as slow and quiet as ever when he said, "You were no daughter of theirs, Mistress. They saw you, straying from your home when you were no more than five years old and stole you for their evil ends, having no child of their own to teach the ways of thieves and rascals."

"Where did they find me? From whom did they steal me?" Cicely held her breath. Would he know? Could he tell her who she really was?

"That they wouldn't say, lass, as you should know. They'd give no man that knowledge to hold over them."

She nodded and walked a little away from them, battling her disappointment. Dickon started to go after her, to comfort her, but Robin caught his arm and said, "Let her be, Dickon. She's a stout lass and she'll not thank you for discovering her tears."

Dickon turned instead to John Howland. "Thank you again, friend," he said and gripped Howland's shoulder hard. "Good fortune follow you in your new life. And if ever I can do you a good turn, command me."

Howland grinned again. He thought it unlikely they ever would meet again. "God go with you, Master Dickon, and with your companions. Look to yourself and the lass."

He turned away and was gone from them, almost before they could draw breath.

CHAPTER XII

Deptford

Dickon and Robin stood watching John Howland until he slipped through the thorn hedge and disappeared.

"He's gone," Robin said, needlessly.

Dickon laughed. "So it seems." He turned toward Cicely. She had herself in hand now and gave him a sad, small smile and said, "There goes a truly gentle man."

"Amen to that," Robin said. "Now what's to do, Dickon?"

"Do?" Dickon's thoughts had been following John Howland. Dull-witted or not, that was a man he'd be proud to call friend. He wished he could have done something really to show his thanks. He'd thought of offering one of the coins Ned Alleyn had given him but instinct warned him against such an action. Silently, he wished John Howland well and turned his mind to Robin's question.

"Do?" he repeated. "Make all speed to London or.
. . ." He broke off and said to Cicely, "Let me have
that letter to Mistress Alleyn. If it be true as John
Howland says that all who can are leaving London
while there's plague, it may be we should look for Mistress Alleyn elsewhere. I'd given no thought before to
the superscription."

Cicely handed him the squared paper and he peered
at the unfamiliar handwriting. Robin came closer and
looked over his shoulder. "To Mistress Joan Alleyn,"
he read, "who is lodged next the Church of St. Nicholas in Deptford Green."

"How can you read the writing?" Dickon asked.
"I've seldom seen worse."

"Habit," Robin said.

"So," Dickon took up his broken sentence, "we'd
best make speed to Deptford and seek out Mistress Alleyn. If we hurry we can, it may be, find her before it's
full dark. Cicely, do you think you can keep a fast pace
for some hours more? Speak true now, girl."

"You'll have no need to hang back for me, Dickon,"
she said stoutly and hoped she could prove her words
as the day drew toward its close. "We've rested long
enough. Let's get on."

"But what of Sparrow?" Robin asked. "What caution
should we use against the chance he'll try again to do
you and Cicely some harm?"

"I doubt he'll show his face again on the road,"
Dickon said slowly. "Not until we're near London.
For, look you Robin, he knows where we're headed.

He has already failed twice to do me harm. It seems to me logical to suppose he'll seek out his friends before he tries again. Then, likely, he'll lie in wait for us at the house of Master Alleyn."

"We're safe enough then," Robin agreed. "For he should look for us in London where Ned ordinarily lives."

"Don't be too sure, Robin," Dickon said. "It would, likely, be no great task to find where Mistress Alleyn is lodging in plague time for, from what you say, there must be many in London who follow the great Alleyn's every move. But this much I do grant. I doubt Sparrow will nose out our whereabouts this night. So we'll likely be safe enough and can make the better speed today if we don't have to keep our eyes and ears always alert for him."

"Why do we wait, then?" Cicely asked and mounted her horse and turned toward the road.

Dickon and Robin followed close behind her and they edged their way among the road people crowded along the edge of the way, until they could put their horses to the gallop. They rode steadily, not speaking, for some time before Robin, again in the lead, slowed and held up his hand.

"Better breathe the nags awhile," he said and led the others aside. "We'll make poor haste if we wear them out and come hobbling to the last miles. If my memory serves me well, there's a stream runs close by the road a little way ahead. We'll rest there and let the horses drink."

Cicely said, "I would be glad of a drink myself," and Dickon echoed, "And I. Riding's thirsty work. Have we made good time, Robin?"

"Good enough." Robin looked at the sun. "We should be at Deptford Green before the night catches us. See, there's my stream."

They guided the horses toward the rivulet that gurgled and chuckled over stones clearly seen beneath the shining, rippled surface of the water. The tired animals, catching its cool scent, walked more quickly and when they were free of their riders drank, thirstily snuffling. When they had done, they began to crop the fresh, new green of the bushes seeming to sense this was a resting time.

Cicely knelt on the bank, upstream of the horses. She cupped her two hands and, leaning far out, poured handful after handful down her parched throat. Dickon and Robin watched her for a moment, enjoying her satisfaction, before they knelt beside her. When she had drunk all she wanted, she sat back on her haunches and watched the water flowing. It held a feeling of peace, of leisure, and she wished she could lie down beside it and sleep for hours and hours. She was, in truth, sick of riding through the countryside as if the devil were up behind her belaboring the mare. And on so fair a day, too! She stretched out her legs and lay upon her back, staring up into the brilliance of the sky, empty blue except for a line of soft, white, cumulous clouds drifting low on the horizon. Fair-weather clouds, she thought, and was glad for all the road folk that tomorrow would, likely, be another good day. There were things she'd miss about the road. She'd miss the feeling of comradeship and the freedom to come and go even as the wind. But it was a hard life and, on the whole, she would be glad to be quit of it. She closed her eyes the better to enjoy these few minutes of resting.

Beside her Dickon and Robin talked quietly. "By rights I should be in Warwickshire with Peter," Dickon said.

"What would you do in Warwickshire, Dickon, with Tom dead and all your goods and chattels sold for his debts? I reckon your hope to end your days as a Cambridge scholar has already gone up the wind of Tom's misfortunes. You could scarcely spend your life as a ploughman on what had been your own land, nor yet as a pensioner of your former servant."

"Not willingly," Dickon said. "Indeed, Robin, I don't know what I would have done, nor what I shall do, if it comes to that, when we have found Marlowe and warned him."

"I doubt you've cause to worry," Robin said. "You have a fine voice for speaking lines and, in the old days, you used to have a way upon the stage. These plague years won't go on forever. Alleyn says the evil is already abating and the autumn will surely see the reopening of all the playhouses. He and his wife's stepfather, Phillip Henslowe, are already planning the winter season at The Rose and he's heard of plans the Burbages are making for their company. And Alleyn predicts there'll be such a rebirth of interest in the theater as not all the whining reformers will be able to put down."

"The Rose?" Dickon asked.

"The theater Master Henslowe most used before the sickness closed them all. With Marlowe's plays and the pick of actors, Alleyn thinks we can make a profitable undertaking of the playhouse that will bring us all riches. And he'll make you a member of his company I'm sure, if you should want it."

Dickon said, "Since I can't spend the rest of my days at Cambridge, there's nothing I'd like better, for it's true I did love the stage in those days before you left the university. But I doubt I can wait until autumn, for I must find some way to put a roof over my head and food in my belly right now."

"Don't be dull-witted, Dickon," Robin said sharply, having little patience with Dickon's pessimism. "That jewel of yours, when it's sold, will keep you well enough I'd vow. It's no cheap bauble, you know. And if it doesn't, you can surely find work as copyist for one of the stationers in Paul's churchyard. You write a clear hand as I recall and there's always work for such a person. Nor would I let you starve, sweet Dickon, while my father has more wealth than he can use. He's no niggardly miser, I can tell you, and would gladly see you through the summer."

"But I could not. . . ." Dickon began.

Robin said, "Have done, Dickon. You'd do as much for me were our states reversed. Once I heard a wise

man say of such things, 'From each according to his
ability; to each according to his need.' Remember that,
and stow your pride and your worrying and we'll say
no more about it. Look. Cicely's asleep and we've been
long enough a-resting. Wake the girl while I gather
the horses."

The rest had done them good and they rode steadily
for what was left of the afternoon. As the sun slid
down the sky toward the western horizon the crowds
upon the road began to thin as first one, then another
individual or group turned aside to make ready for
sleeping. Few of the foot travelers wanted to come by
night to London.

Cicely was beginning to feel again the ache and exhaustion in her body. She shut her teeth hard together
and prepared to endure misery, determined not to let
any sound betray her this time, to Dickon. She hoped
Mistress Alleyn could command hot water as Mistress
Rose had done. Her body longed for that comfort. She
thought she'd been riding since time began, and would
go on riding until time ended or until her leg muscles,
locked against the mare's flanks, gave way and she tumbled into the road dust. How far, oh heaven, how far
had they still to ride?

Robin turned and said, "Look!" and she followed
his pointing finger and saw ahead, ranged against the
purple and green afterglow of the sunset, a fairy army
of spires marching in serried lines toward the dark.

"Is it London?" Dickon asked.

"What else?" Robin said. "Half an hour should see us in Deptford."

Dickon drew alongside Cicely and said, "Hold hard, girl. The riding's almost done and then you can rest."

"Yes," she agreed. She wouldn't say any more, wouldn't use for prattle energy that she needed for this final stretch.

Dickon seemed to understand for he kept his silence. He had a fine, gentle soul, she thought, and this time did not laugh at the idea of a gentle spirit in that body so apt for fighting if need arose. She would hate to leave him. He had, this day, roused in her emotions she'd never felt before. She tried to put a name to them. Admiration! She'd not before felt admiration for any man though she'd liked one or two of the scoundrels who had been her companions for ten dreary years. But it was more than that. Tenderness? She wondered. She couldn't tell. Though she'd heard the word often enough she'd found no sign of it in her experience. She gave it up and bent all her mind to enduring these last few miles.

Dickon, watching her, knew she was nearing the end of her tether. He wanted to find words to bring her strength and comfort and could think of none. Just as well. She would, likely, do better alone. She had courage, did this child of the road. And grace of mind as well as of body. When they were wed. . . .

He nearly lost his grip on the racing horse. What had he thought? Wed Cicely! Why he hardly knew her. But quite suddenly and clearly he was sure he did love her, sure he would wed her, if she would have him. Robin had been right there on the stairs at the posting house. Robin and John Howland, who had called Cicely "your lady." Well then, so be it. He knew his own heart now and the knowledge gave him a new direction. For the first time since Tom had died the icy feeling of loneliness left him. In its place hope for the future began to grow; hope and purpose to find a real place for himself in the unknown, bustling world of London. A place for himself and, please heaven, for Cicely.

The sunset's afterglow still lingered as Robin's shout announced their destination reached. "We're here!" he called, and Cicely lifted her tired head and saw the scattering of houses that announced the beginning of Deptford.

Dickon laid a hand upon the mare's rein and slowed the animal. Cicely straightened her back as she and Dickon came, at a walk, to take their places beside Robin.

"The Church of St. Nicholas is but a few streets ahead," Robin said. "Let's go there and find where Joan Alleyn is lodged. Then I'll take the horses to Simon Smith, as Joel bade us, while you explain to Joan the chance that brings us to her."

He looked at Cicely and leaned to pat her on the knee. "Well done, girl," he said. "You are, in truth, stout of heart."

Cicely managed a smile for him, knowing this was,

from Robin, both high praise and a kind of apology for his past complaints about her weakness.

Slowly, picking their way through night-deserted streets and lanes where filthy streams ran at each edge, they went toward Deptford Green. For a moment or two the noisome stench made Cicely feel a little sick and she swallowed again and again to down the nausea that made her want to retch. But her nose adjusted quickly to the evil-smelling waste and by the time they came to the Green she had forgotten it.

"There's the Church of St. Nicholas," Robin said, pointing ahead to a square, buttressed stone tower that reared out of the gloom. On one side of the tower there was what looked to be an empty space of land which Dickon guessed to be the churchyard. On the other side he could just make out a half-timbered house that reminded him of Stratford on Avon where Tom had taken him long ago. Robin was turning his horse toward the house. Dickon said, "I'll knock and inquire for Mistress Alleyn." Robin nodded and held Dickon's reins while he dismounted and went to the door.

He was back in a little more than a minute. "It's the right house," he said, "and Mistress Alleyn's within. I gave the letter to a little serving maid to take to her. Come, Cicely."

He reached up for her and, in spite of her protestations that she could manage well enough by herself, lifted her down from the mare.

"I'll be with you shortly," Robin said and led the two riderless horses away.

Cicely said, "Give me a moment, Dickon, to steady my legs."

He put his arms about her while she flexed the muscles. "Cicely," he said. "Cicely, I. . . ."

She turned to peer full at him in the light from the still open door and knew she was seeing him, really seeing him, for the first time. Light ringed his head with a nimbus of gold and picked out flecks of gold in his brown eyes that shone with the thoughts that lay behind them. He was, certainly, not a handsome man, she thought. His nose turned up a little and his mouth was too wide for beauty. But the face was dearer to her than any face she'd ever known or dreamed of. She wondered how such a thing could be when she'd known him but a few days. Strange. He was watching her eyes as if he were breathless, waiting for some sign.

Sign of what, she wondered. And suddenly, as if she had been struck by a bolt of lightning from a cloudless sky, she felt her whole self stilled and rigid.

She recognized now the new emotion that had ridden with her all this long day. She remembered summer nights beside the road when a wandering minstrel played love songs upon his lute or a down-at-heels scholar made the night throb with tales of lovers dead, long gone but remembered for their loving—Aucassin and Nicolette, Lancelot and Guinevere, Paolo and Francesca. She'd listened and laughed and wept according to the ending of the tales. She'd thought she'd

known what they were about. Now she knew she'd felt
no more than a shadow of the meaning of the songs
and the stories. Now she was gripped and wrung by
the very substance of love itself and she thought the
tenderness and longing, the sweetness and the bitter
pain would rack her heart in two.

Dickon said again, "Cicely!" and she reached up and
laid her hand gently upon his lips not wanting, for the
moment, even his words to break in upon this new realization of her womanhood. I love him, her mind was
saying over and over. Oh, how I love him!

Then, as suddenly as the glory had come to her, it
gave way to despair. What good could come of this?
She was a nothing, a child of the road, a hoyden, a
thief. And Dickon—Dickon, her Dickon was a gentleman, to the manner born, a scholar, a member of that
class to which she thought she too rightly belonged.
But what good was thinking? What good was feeling
sure in her own mind? There was no proof. Nor ever
would be. Her body sagged away from him as she
dropped her fingers and turned her head so he
couldn't see her eyes.

He said, for the third time, "Cicely!" and it seemed
to her ears a cry of anguish. So he knew it, too. Knew
there was no hope for them, no future together.

When she made no response to him he sensed some
deep trouble in her and put his arms about her and
forced her resisting body close to him.

"No, Dickon," she cried, "don't."

"But, Cicely," he spoke softly and gently, "don't you

understand? I love you, sweeting. Will you wed with me?"

For a moment she stayed where she was, savoring the sweetness. Then she jerked away from him and blurted words. "No! No! No! Dickon, I can't. I can't."

He was at once startled by her vehemence and hurt and affronted by it. "Oh," he said stiffly, "I had thought. . . ."

She turned to him then, turned into the light which discovered to him the tears upon her face. At once the hurt and affront disappeared and he reached out toward her and said, "My love, my little love, what is it? What distresses you so?"

"How can I wed you, Dickon? How can I? If John Howland had known more of me—if he could have named my true parents and given me a proper place in the world and—and a name—then I would have married you with all the joy in the world. For I do love you, Dickon. But I cannot. I cannot come to you nameless and stained with all the evils of the road."

He wanted to shout his relief into the night, wanted to dance and sing for joy. Instead he spoke quietly and soberly, reasoning with her, careful not to distress her by his delight. Not now. Not until he had driven away the dark night of her doubt and fear. Then they could laugh together.

"Look at me, Cicely." He lifted her chin again until her eyes were upon his. "Do you think I care for a name? Or a place of importance in the world? No.

Wait, my girl, my love. There's no one left in my family to care who or what you are. Not that that would have mattered to me! I'm my own man and I can make my own life without let or hindrance or even any fuss. I'll give you a name. My own. Cicely Fontayne. How do you like the sound of that?"

"But. . . ."

"No. There are no buts. Listen. As for those stains from the road—they are already cleansed. Nor were they, I'll warrant, ever more than skin deep. Gentleness isn't a matter of high birth or rich parents, but a thing that lives inside you. It's who you are, you yourself, that matters, not where you spring from or the names and station of your family."

He reached out and took off the cap she'd been wearing and ruffled the shorn curls. "For the matter of that," he went on and grimaced at her. "I'm not so much myself—homeless, landless, all but pennyless and with few prospects for the future except my own will to make a place in the world. For us, Cicely. Shall we begin again, all equal? I love you, sweeting. Will you wed me?"

For another small moment she held herself from him, frowning, thinking of the things he had said and trying to weigh them in fairness to him. Then, with a joyful, small cry she nodded her head. "That I will, Dickon Fontayne. My love. My love."

He reached out for her to take her in his arms, but he had barely touched her shoulder when the serving maid was back at the door. "Come," she called. "The mistress is waiting."

Cicely whispered, "Later, my Dickon."

He gave her shoulder a hard squeeze and dropped his hand to take her arm. Together they walked into the light, their hearts and faces joyful.

CHAPTER XIII

Mistress Alleyn

"I'm to take you straightaway to Mistress Alleyn, Master." The serving maid stood aside to let them enter ahead of her. She started to close the door behind them and opened it wide again and looked into the night as a distant voice called, "Wait! Dickon. Wait for me!"

She turned and looked a question at Dickon and he laughed and nodded his head. "All's well," he said. "It's another of us back from seeing to our horses. So, Robin," he added as Robin Lang came, panting a little for he had been running hard, into the narrow hallway, "you made quick work of that."

"It wasn't so far," Robin said as they followed the maid up a crooked stairway, "and I ran all the way back so you would not have to make your explanations to Joan without my help."

"Ho!" Dickon said, feeling now he knew Cicely loved him, as if he would never again need anyone's

help save hers. "Ho! I don't doubt I could have explained well enough without you." Out of his high
spirits he cuffed Robin lightly on the shoulder.

"Now what's come over you, Dickon Fontayne?
Such playfulness atop this long day's journey. I'll
warrant. . . ."

The maid's knock at the door cut off the rest of his
sentence. She gave them a little curtsy and disappeared.

A pleasant low voice from inside called, "Enter,"
and Robin opened the door and went in ahead of
them. He seized the small, graceful lady—no, Dickon
thought, she was little more than a girl—and lifted her
off her feet and swung her about, as if she weighed no
more than thistleseed.

"By the heavens," Robin said, "it's good to see you
again, Joan."

"Put me *down*, Robin Lang," Joan Alleyn ordered.
"Put me down and tell me of my Ned."

"He's well and sends you his love, puss," Robin still
held her tightly.

"Leave be, Robin you goose," she said and looked
toward the doorway where Dickon and Cicely watched
Robin's antics with amusement. "Would you have me
keep your friends standing before my door all night?
What would Ned say to such hospitality?"

Robin set her down and she settled her blue velvet
gown and came toward Dickon and Cicely, smiling a
welcome. "Come in, young gentlemen. . . ."

She broke off and stared a long moment at Cicely

before she turned back to Robin, her face tight. "Is this another of your madcap pranks, Robin, or—or something worse? Ned said nothing of a young lady."

Robin had come to stand beside her. He grinned at Cicely and said, mockingly, "It seems the masquerade is over, Mistress."

Cicely drew herself as tall as she could and glared at him. Why did Robin still want to mock her? Was it because of Dickon? Because Robin was afraid she would, in some measure, rob him of part of his friend's affection? Stupid!

Dickon put his hand on her arm and propelled her into the room. Joan Alleyn moved into the room a little, her back poker-stiff, the smile gone from her face. "Robin!" she said and the word was a demand for an explanation.

"Softly, Joan," Robin said. "We'll make everything clear in good time. But we've ridden hard this day and are tired and thirsty."

She relaxed a little, remembering her manners, and gestured toward chairs. "Sit down and I will fetch ale for you."

While she went to the tall chest that stood in one corner of the room and held flagons and her supply of ale, Dickon looked about the spacious chamber well lit with a ceiling candelabra that blazed with wax candles. Cicely had dropped into a high-backed chair, grateful for the cushions that padded it, achingly aware of her tiredness. Robin was wandering about the room like a cat in a new place. Dickon went to stand behind

Cicely, reaching around the chairback to put a hand on her shoulder. He was puzzled and uncertain because of Mistress Alleyn's attitude. He had, he realized, counted on her cooperation in the matter of Cicely. Now he was not so sure, for she seemed to hold his girl in low esteem. Why?

Mistress Alleyn came back to them with the ale and gave each of them a flagon. "Now, Robin Lang," she said and her voice held no warmth, "will you tell me of this—this *lady*—or should I say your doxy?"

Cicely spoke then. Her voice was as cold as Mistress Alleyn's and full of dignity. "You've no cause to mock me, Mistress. I am a lady—a lady born and this I know though I have no proof. My life has been filled with misfortune though that, thank heaven, is over. Dickon and, later, Robin befriended me and brought me here. But I'll not trouble you long, for I'll be off again as soon as the ale is done and I have rested a little."

Dickon said, "Cicely. . . ," and in the same breath Joan Alleyn, looking a little shamed, said, "Alack, Mistress Cicely, I did not mean to mock you. I—it's. . . ."

Robin said, "Be quiet, all of you and let us waste no more time. Cicely stop bristling. You're overtired. Joan sit down and listen. Dickon, it's your tale. Tell it."

Dickon began, he hoped for the last time, the story of Tom's death and of all the events that had followed upon it.

When he had finished, Joan Alleyn came to Cicely's chair. She pushed Dickon aside and knelt on the floor beside it and took Cicely's hand. "Why you're nothing but a poor, lost little ewe lamb," she said, "with nobody but men for comfort. Decking you out in boy's clothes, when any fool can see by the face and the body on you, you're a maid and a fair one at that! I've no doubt you are well born and stolen away though there's no hope we'll ever find your parents now. Not that it matters for we'll look after you, my Ned and I."

Cicely, more and more aware of the aches in her body and the tiredness in her mind, didn't know whether to laugh or cry. Ewe lamb indeed! What would this Mistress Alleyn say could she know the whole of Cicely's story? She said, "I . . . I. . . ," and couldn't go on.

Dickon came to her rescue. "We do thank you, Mistress Alleyn, Cicely and I. And I'll be most grateful if you would look after my—my girl till I can find work. She and I plan to wed when. . . ."

"Sits the wind in that quarter?" Robin put in. "Not that I'm surprised and I am, most truly, pleased for both of you. It does seem a pity to turn away from so happy a thought. But we have other, serious things, dire things perhaps, to consider."

Joan Alleyn looked at him. "Serious things, Robin? What could be more serious, and more joyful, than a wedding?"

"Have you forgotten Ned's letter, Joan? Or did he

not speak of the danger to Christopher Marlowe? If it were not for that business we should none of us be here."

She clapped her hands to her face and her look of dismay was so comic the others laughed aloud. "I had forgotten," she said. "How could I? My Ned said something is amiss with Kit Marlowe and I'm to help you. He said he was in a hurry—and that's no news for he usually is—and you would explain. So—but wait. Whatever is wrong with Marlowe, there's nothing can be done till tomorrow. And you must be near to starving. I'll send the serving maid for supper. And bespeak a chamber for you, Robin and your friend, Dickon Fontayne is it? As for you, my Cicely, we'll soon have you out of those ridiculous clothes and into a tub of hot water. Then, when you're all rested a little and fed, we'll talk of Marlowe."

Later the four of them sat about an empty table, relaxed and smiling. Joan Alleyn, once Cicely was soaking her tired body in a steaming wooden tub, had bustled about arranging with the owner of the house for a bed for Robin and Dickon, packing them off to wash themselves and change their travel-stained clothes, sending the maid servant to the nearest tavern for food. Robin had found in his boxes suitable clothes for Dickon and they had settled to their changing with few words, realizing how tired they were, now they were settled for the night and had time to relax.

They had come back to Joan Alleyn's rooms and

Dickon had caught his breath at the sight of Cicely. The bath had indeed refreshed her. The skin of her face glowed with happiness and well-being. She looked as if she could never stop smiling. Joan had brushed her shorn hair until it made a halo of copper light about her small, neat head and dressed her in one of her own gowns of green velvet picked out with gold. The slight, uncertain boy had turned into a young woman of great beauty and dignity.

They were all hungry and they had fallen upon the cold roast fowl and new-baked bread without more urging, holding their talk until their appetites were satisfied. Then Robin pushed back his chair and patted his full stomach and let out a long ah-h-h-h of satisfaction. He looked at each of them in turn and grinned. But he was, at once, sober-faced again. "Now," he said, "we must think about Kit Marlowe and his danger. If he *is* in danger."

Joan Alleyn frowned and sighed. "There's likely to be truth in it, Robin," she said. "Headlong Kit Marlowe. His mind is always in the clouds and his thoughts upon the music of his words. He's no time left over for everyday considerations. I could wish he had more caution in him and less willingness to act upon swift anger. Heaven knows he's in trouble enough already with the Queen's council, though I doubt they'll do more than question him since they didn't put him at once in prison. But I don't, quite, see why anyone would go about and plan to kill him."

"Could someone—someone who fears what Marlowe knows of them, fear also just such questioning by the council? If he were put to the rack. . . ?" Robin didn't finish the sentence. He didn't need to. Joan Alleyn nodded her head, trouble in her eyes.

"Yes," she said. "There could be something in that, for no man knows what bitter secrets Marlowe carries in his head. I doubt even the rack could force him to reveal anything that would bring harm to his friends. But these are troubled times and his enemies. . . . They are numerous as the acorns in autumn. They may indeed be afraid, for I doubt if any rack would be needed to get our Kit to say what he knows of them if it be anything aimed at the safety of the Queen or the country. If we only knew who they were!"

"We have three names of rascally men who may be, in some manner, connected with Marlowe," Dickon said. "One Frizer—and I don't know whether that's a first name or a last—and a man named Skeres and one named Poley, possibly Robert Poley, though we can't be sure."

Joan frowned. "I've no knowledge of Frizer or yet of Skeres. Robert Poley, if your man be he, is known to Marlowe. Not so long ago Kit was forced to kill a man —in fair fight and to save his own life. But, before the law absolved him of guilt, he spent a time in prison. This Poley, too, was in the jail and there he taught Kit the ways of coining. And once when Kit had had too much wine he even boasted he could make as fine coins as ever came from the Queen's mint. And never think that idle boast has not been quoted against him by his enemies! Kit Marlowe a coiner! The absurdity of it. But whether Poley is friend or foe I can't say."

"Ned would say he's friend to no man but himself," Robin said.

"Ned doesn't like him, nor trust him. Oh, I wish Ned were here. He knows Kit Marlowe so much better than I."

Cicely had been sitting, listening quietly to all their talk. Now she spoke, and the other three jumped for even Dickon had, for the moment, forgotten her. "It seems to me," she said, "it makes little profit to sit wondering who is friend and who enemy to this Master Marlowe. Surely he will know who is which. If Dickon and Robin can find him and give him their warning, Dickon will have discharged his promise to his brother, they will both have done what they could, and the rest will be up to Master Marlowe himself."

"The girl has sense," Robin said approvingly. "Where does he keep himself now in plague time, Joan? Ned thought he'd surely have left his London lodgings."

"Maybe he went home to Canterbury," Dickon suggested.

Robin shook his head. "No, for the sickness rages even more violently there than here and his father, John Marlowe, has his house and his tannery within the walls, not like my father, in the clean country air. So, where should we look for him, Joan?"

Joan Alleyn pinched her lips between her two fingers. "I've not seen him these weeks past," she said.

"But he cannot be far from London since he's under orders to present himself without delay to the council when they shall be pleased to question him about this charge of atheism the rascal Kyd laid upon him. Oh, why has Marlowe not the good sense to keep silent upon such grave matters as the nature of the godhead? I've heard him accused of popery as well as atheism."

" 'The mind must be still climbing after infinite and always moving with the spheres,' " Dickon quoted softly in the little pause that followed her outburst.

"Why, that's a line from *Tamburlaine*," Joan Alleyn said. "How many times have I heard my Ned speaking it, now this way, now that, to get the best effect? But —but. . . ."

"I know all his works," Dickon explained, "for I have a good memory for poetry and I never missed a chance to hear his plays when they were given in inns near Cambridge. His own words prove him a seeker after one thing only—the very truth. I doubt such a man would ever guard his tongue or fear to read in whatever books interested him, no matter what their content."

Robin said, "Amen to that," and added dryly, "nor will he, likely, take heed to our warning. Still we must try. *But* we must find him first."

Joan said, "My best guess is he would go to Scadbury and Thomas Walsingham for he is Walsingham's man. Scadbury is not so far from London he could not readily answer the council's summons when it comes.

And it's safe enough from the sickness for, like Robin's home, it's in clean country air."

"Then that's where we'll look for him tomorrow," Dickon said, and reached over to take Cicely's hand. "As for you, sweeting," he went on, "do you think Mistress Joan will share her bed with you this night?"

"That I will and gladly," Joan said. "So let us all go to our beds now and meet again to break our fast in the morning. Then, while you, Dickon, and Robin go to Scadbury, Cicely and I will spend our waiting time upon women's affairs."

Robin got up and stretched. Cicely half smothered a yawn. Dickon leaned over her, not caring that he was overlooked by Robin and Joan, and kissed her gently on the mouth. "Shall I carry you, sweeting?" he asked. "You do look weary."

She laughed at him and said, "That you shall not, Dickon. Tired I may be, but not too tired to take myself to bed. Shall we go, Mistress Joan?"

Joan put an arm about Cicely's shoulders and started with her toward the bed chamber. At the door she turned, gave Cicely a little push to send her on ahead and said, "I had forgotten one other thing, Dickon. My Ned spoke of a jewel you want to sell and bade me get a good price for it."

Dickon, too, had forgotten the ring. He lifted it upon its thong and took it off and handed it to her. She held it a moment, turning it this way and that, watching the sparkling lines of color it sent out as the

light caught now this facet, now that of the rubies sur-
rounded by diamonds. "Why, it's worth a fortune," she
said.

"It was my mother's," Dickon explained. "She gave
it to Tom to keep for me when she was near dying. It's
all that's left of my father's wealth. Would you keep it
a while? If, as Robin thinks, I can find work with some
company of players when autumn comes and keep myself meantime as copyist to a stationer, I'd like to save
the ring for Cicely."

"That I will, Dickon Fontayne. And don't be afraid
for your future. Ned thinks there's wealth to be made
in playhouses once they reopen. I'll write him this very
night and speak for you as player and shareholder in
The Rose and there'll be no trouble I promise. Now a
good night to you both. Sleep well and be up betimes
in the morning."

CHAPTER XIV

Scadbury Manor

"Tomorrow," Robin said as he and Dickon, mounted on fresh horses, rode toward Scadbury in a morning still sparkling with last night's dew, "tomorrow will be the first day of June and my birthday."

Dickon grunted. He wondered that Robin could think of such things now. For himself, he could give his mind to nothing but the need for haste.

The horses' hooves beat the refrain, Mar-*lowe*, Mar-*lowe*. Mar-*lowe*. They must find him. They must warn him. In the days since Tom's death his own deep admiration for the poet had doubled with thinking until he had come almost to feel as if he and Christopher Marlowe were one; more, as if Marlowe stood for something so important, so rare in the world of Queen Elizabeth that all England would, in some degree, suffer if harm should come to this man who had given, through his search for truth and his mighty lines of poetry, a whole new dimension to thought. Beside him, the other poets of the day were mere rhymesters, scribbling nothings. If Marlowe had taken no thought for his danger. . . .

"Hurry," he said and pricked his already galloping horse to an even faster pace.

They had risen early, refreshed and well rested from all the excitements of yesterday, determined to find Marlowe and persuade him to take care. Joan and Cicely had joined them as they broke their fast with a joint of cold beef and ale fresh from the brew house. It had seemed to Dickon then that Cicely had been transformed in the night; changed in some subtle way that reminded him of the Roman Ovid's stories he'd read at the parson's school at Chipping Norton. It was not only that in another, different gown of Joan Alleyn's her external parts were apt for a lady. It was, over and beyond this change in her looks, a thing within her that had altered. A certain coarseness of manner left upon her by the road life had, it appeared, been lost while she slept, in the new-found knowledge of their love. He found it hard to believe he had ever threatened this girl to keep her from stealing! Her eyes that had been sullen and wary at times, and always secret as if they would protect her spirit from some violence, were wide open now and eager, ready to send her thoughts gladly to meet another's thoughts. And that gaiety he'd seen in flashes, she now seemed to wear as a garment touched with radiance that came from deep inside her mind.

While Joan Alleyn had described to Robin the shor-

test way they should ride to Scadbury, Dickon and
Cicely had sat apart in the window seat and spoken together, saying over and over the soft, nonsense words
of lovers. He could not, now, remember what they had
said, but the tenderness of their mutual loving held
him still in thrall and he knew the words they had
used mattered not a whit.

When Robin had the directions clearly in his mind
they had left the house beside the church and ridden
along the Thames bank, seeing across its water the
crowding streets and lanes of London. Dickon had
thought, though he knew it could not be so, that he
could actually see the noxious pall of the plague, as if
it were the miasma rising from some foul swampy
place, hanging over the city. A hundred church bells
rang the hour as they passed. The ragged clanging,
muted a little by distance, seemed to have a dismal
sound as if each were a passing bell. As, he thought,
each was, for every hour men and women and children
were dying of the sickness. He touched the little sprigs
of rue and herb-of-grace Joan Alleyn had tucked beneath the plain ruff about his neck. Joan had taken the
sprigs from pots in her window. Her dear Ned, she
had explained, had warned her to keep them there as a
guard against the plague should it succeed in crossing
Thames water.

When Robin announced this to be his birthday eve,
they had been riding for an hour and had covered
most of the way to their destination. Robin looked
around at Dickon's order. "No need to counsel hurry,

now, Dickon," he said, "for yonder must be the lane that leads straight to Scadbury Manor."

A wide avenue, lined each side with ancient beech trees branched off from the road a little way in front of them. Already, the new copper-colored leaves dappled the ground with shade that would grow more welcome as the day grew older. For the sun, even so early in the morning, was warmer than ordinary for the coming of June and it would be too hot for comfort as the hours stretched toward noon.

The way led straight for as far as the eye could follow toward a silvery sheet Dickon guessed to be the great moat that spread like a lake about Scadbury Manor. Joan Alleyn had told them something about the place. It was a sprawling house, begun more than two hundred years ago as a fortified castle and added to by little and little as the fortunes and the families of the Walsinghams increased, until now it stood, part gray, forbidding stone; part the warm half-timbered apartments that had come into fashion with the Tudor kings.

As they came closer they could see the house and its reflection in the lakelike moat where pads of water lilies awaited their freight of white flowers that would come later in the summer. Dickon caught his breath at the sight and, as if with one thought, he and Robin urged their horses forward. They came quickly to the ancient drawbridge, once a vital part of the castle's defense when the houses of Lancaster and York fought for the right to rule England. No longer needed, since King Henry the Seventh had brought domestic peace once again to the land and the people, the drawbridge was now no more than a way to cross the moat. He doubted if it had been raised in three generations.

Their horses' hooves clattered across the bridge under the rusting portcullis above their heads and into a stone-paved courtyard. The place was swarming with people. Farmers dickered with stewards over the price of eggs and vegetables. Servants moved up and down a flight of stone stairs from the kitchens with food for a long, trestle table set along one side of the yard near a stone wall. Great joints of beef, sides of mutton, a whole suckling pig with an apple in its mouth, were upon the boards along with loaves of bread and wooden bowls holding other foods Dickon could only guess at. Men of many stations in life stood about the table which seemed to be open to all comers. Some of them were splendidly dressed after the latest fashion of the court. Some wore the Walsingham livery. Others were soberly garbed in the manner of merchants. All, or so it seemed, were talking at the very tops of their voices. The noise was deafening and the confusion distracting. No one in the yard paid the least attention to Dickon and Robin who sat upon their horses trying to find someone who seemed to be in authority.

Robin said at last, "What a babel. Zounds! Let us look in a quieter place for someone to question. The stables must be nearby."

Dickon agreed and they found a bridle path that cir-
cled the outside walls of the manor. They had not far
to go before the pathway branched away toward a
clump of oaks that sheltered a series of smaller buildings. They could hear the stamp of horses and one of
their own mounts neighed and began to trot rapidly
toward the trees.

The quiet outbuildings seemed to be deserted.
Robin cupped his hands about his mouth and shouted,
"Hola! Is there no one about to see to the horses when
friends come riding to Scadbury Manor?"

Almost at once a boy's head appeared around the
door of one of the buildings. "Faith and you do be in a
rush," he said impudently when he saw that Robin
and Dickon were little older than he. He came to them
and held their horses. "If you come to see Master Walsingham," he continued, "you'd as well go back the
way you came for he's gone to Windsor to see the
Queen. Or so he said. Myself, I'd wager he's gone off
a-courting his lady, Mistress Audrey, since he's a man
near besotted with love for the chit. But, gone he is for
he came storming after his favorite stallion before the
sun was over the hill and rode off as if the devil were
following. He. . . ."

"Have done," Robin said impatiently. "We have no
business with Master Walsingham. We seek his man,
Christopher Marlowe, who. . . ."

"Christopher Marlowe is it?" The stableboy spat into
the dust as if he would rid himself of the taste of an

evil word. "The devil take that one for a God-hater and a murderer. If it's him you're after you'll get no help from me for I do run and hide when I see him coming, in case he puts the devil's mark upon me." He extended his hand, doubled into a fist except for the first and little fingers which stuck straight out in the age-old sign against the evil eye. "And do you not think but he can call the devil to his aid and it pleases him? A conjuror he is and a blasphemer and a coiner to boot and the saints only. . . ."

"Hold your lying tongue!" Dickon said angrily. "Have you never learned manners that you speak evil of your betters. Evil and nonsense! I. . . ."

"Dickon!" Robin said, quietly enough, but there was that in his voice that commanded silence. "So, you don't know Master Marlowe's whereabouts, boy? Who will know, then?"

The boy muttered to himself, scowling a little and didn't answer Robin's question.

"Well?" Robin said. "Answer me if you don't relish the stick across your back." His mild voice had taken on depth and authority and Dickon thought he sounded almost as if he were a king giving orders to an underling.

"Likely the chief steward or the housekeeper," the boy answered sullenly, backing away from Robin.

"And where will I find the one or the other?" With an effort Robin kept the rising impatience out of his words. Master Walsingham was ill served, he thought.

"How would I know? I'm nothing but a stableboy and not welcome at the house. Find them for yourselves."

He jerked the reins of the horses and ran with them toward the stable.

"'There," Robin said as he and Dickon turned back along the path, "there's the kind of superstitious dolt would stick a knife in Marlowe's back as soon as bid him God speed—if he were less afraid of the devil! The saints preserve us from his like."

"Why did you suffer his talk? He needs a beating to teach him manners."

Robin shrugged. "Dickon, Dickon," he said, "you're too quick to anger. You can't go about beating other men's servants. Besides, if you'd kept on at him, we'd have had not one more word from him. Not that we got much help as it is!" Robin finished with a grin so impish it restored Dickon to good humor.

They came again to hubbub in the courtyard and Robin, taking the lead, began to shoulder a passage for them through the crowd, making his way toward the table and a tall man, neatly dressed in black, who stood near it. The man was reading from a sheaf of papers he held in his hand and seemed unaware of the confusion all about him.

Robin said, "Isn't it Master Blount, the stationer?"

The man went on reading, his lips moving as if he pronounced each word silently to himself.

"Sir?" Robin said and when the man still did not answer, touched his arm. The man started a little and

turned toward Robin, looking mazed, Dickon thought,
as if he had been recalled from some far place.

> ". . . so wondrous fair,
> So young, so gentle and so debonair,"

he read aloud and seemed really to see Robin for the
first time and came back from whatever other world
he'd been in and said, "Was ever finer description of a
young heroine? Ah, Marlowe, Marlowe, what a very
wizard with words you are! And how may I help you,
young man?"

Robin gulped. "I recognized you, or thought I did,
as Master Edward Blount, printer and stationer of
Paul's churchyard."

"Indeed I am he," Master Blount acknowledged and
bowed and waited.

"We are looking for that Christopher Marlowe you
mentioned," Robin went on. "We were told we might
find him here but we haven't seen him in this motley
crowd. We bring a—a message from an old friend."

"He is here," Edward Blount said, "or was a little
time ago when he gave me these papers." He tapped
the manuscript he held. "It's the beginning of a new
work—a poem called *Hero and Leander*—and a mighty
piece of work it will be when it's finished. And when
that time comes I'll be off to London to hurry it to
print, plague or no plague."

"Do you know where we can find Master Marlowe,
then?" Robin persisted.

"That I do not, young man. I saw him stop to talk

with that scoundrel Ingram Frizer—and I could wish
he would choose his companions more wisely—and
Frizer's shadow that is always with him, and then I
turned to reading the lines and was so lost in a glory of
words I thought of nothing more till you brought me
back to the everyday world. No doubt the steward will
know, for Marlowe must leave word where he may be
reached should a messenger come from the council."

Dickon and Robin had looked at each other when
they had heard the name Ingram Frizer. Dickon had
started to exclaim but Robin pressed his arm and
shook his head to warn against any comment. Dickon
wondered if Robin did not altogether trust this Edward Blount or if he were only convinced this was a
case where least said was soonest mended.

Robin said, "We know of that matter, sir," and
Blount replied, "As does all England by this time I
should think, with the frightened Kyd, may his soul
rot in hell, spilling his mind helter-skelter and accusing Marlowe of dire things to avoid the threatened
rack! What a pother over nothing with Marlowe seized
upon that very bridge there and dragged before the
council and told to wait upon their lordship's pleasure.
Ho! Kit Marlowe an atheist and traitor! As well call
Queen Elizabeth herself such names."

"Indeed, you have the right of it, Master Blount,"
Robin said quickly. "I. . . ."

Dickon was troubled more than ever since the mention of Ingram Frizer, who must surely be the man a

drunken Sparrow had talked about to Jackdaw—and could Skeres be the shadow of Frizer just mentioned? He was feeling the sharp prick of fear for Marlowe. He spoke softly, "Your pardon, Robin, but shouldn't we find this steward and get on with our business?"

Robin's face reddened a little and he said, "Where should we find the steward, Master Blount?"

Blount was clearly impatient now to be back at his reading. He pointed to a door in the stone wall of the house. "That door will take you into the Great Hall. You'll likely find him there, or someone who can tell you where he is."

Dickon was sure the printer did not hear Robin's thanks for he was lost once more in his "glory of words." For a moment Dickon wished he could stay and ask to hear this new work by the greatest poet of them all—or so they called him. But Robin had turned away and started toward the house. Dickon sighed and followed him. Some day, perhaps, he would read the poem for himself. He wondered if it would be as fine as that other, joyous writing he'd learned at Cambridge. The opening lines of it ran now in his head as he edged between the crowded bodies in the courtyard:

> Come live with me and be my love,
> And we shall all the pleasures prove,
> That valleys, grove, hills and fields
> Woods and steep mountain yields.

> And we shall sit upon the rocks
> Seeing the shepherds feed their flocks
> By shallow rivers, to whose falls
> Melodious birds sing madrigals.

He could go no further for his memory forsook him. *The Passionate Shepherd to His Love*—that was the name of it. How he wished he could compose such a work for his love.

"Dickon! You're moon-gathering. Thinking of your Cicely I'll be bound, like any love-sick swain. Wake up!"

Robin was waiting for him beside the door and Dickon steadied his mind for its proper business. He thought (and was amused at himself) he'd lost, with his suddenly discovered love for Cicely, that pride in making decisions that had come to him on the road to London. That kind of pride seemed to matter less now. But he swore to himself he'd not again think of Cicely until Christopher Marlowe had been found and warned.

They pushed open one of the panels of the great double doors that must have been cut from the trunk of a single oak which had stood as long as there had been an England. Each panel was intricately carved by a master craftsman of the olden times, not content to leave the wood bare and plain. Small animals peeped out from wreaths of vine leaves and, here and there, a human face—or a face of a fairy being—grinned at Dickon.

So much he saw and wished he could see more before they were standing within an enormous room that rose up and up to huge beams arching beneath a wooden ceiling. Upon the plastered walls hung paintings in watercolor of strange, half-naked, copper-skinned men cooking fish over fires or dancing before round huts that seemed to be made of twigs. He had heard at the university of the savage creatures Sir Walter Raleigh's colonists had found in the New World across the western ocean. Could these be pictures of Indians?

Thick, white candles stood in triangular iron sconces at intervals between the paintings. Two fireplaces, each holding six-foot logs, smoldered with fires lit, in spite of the outside warmth, against the winter damp that still lingered in the room.

At first they could see no one and Robin looked at Dickon and said, "Now what do we do?" Then they both heard a rustling in the stillness as if a mouse were gnawing behind the plaster; they went toward the sound and came around a carved screen and found an elderly, small man, all wrinkled of face, scratching in an account book with a quill that needed sharpening.

"Well?" The wizened man looked at them, impatient at the interruption.

Robin was staring in fascination at the face as if he would draw the lines in his memory. Dickon said, "We are looking for Master Christopher Marlowe and were. . . ."

"Marlowe, Marlowe, Marlowe," the old man said.

"Curse the man. I rue the time my master befriended him and made him welcome here. Always mooning about with no thought for the trouble he causes. Off to the woods with his paper and his inkpot and his pen stuck in his belt like a street-corner scrivener who'll write whatever you like for a penny. Carving his initials on our finest trees as if he were a lad. Content to pick at the common table outside when my master expects him to sit at meat like a proper gentleman which he's not, being nothing but a tanner's son! Not but what he's generous enough with the money he gets from writing hell-begotten plays of raising the devil, and with his apologies when trouble's been made."

He paused in his headlong prattle and peered at them from small, suspicious, red-rimmed eyes. "Argh —who are you? Do you come from council? No, I see you don't for you're far too young for that business. What is it you want with Marlowe?"

"We bring a message—an urgent message—from a friend," Dickon said.

"Message? Then you'll have to find him for yourselves for he's gone to Deptford. Heard him tell the steward here in this very room above an hour ago and disturbed me at my work the while. How can a man get on with the reckoning of the accounts with such a haloo-balloo about him?"

"Where in Deptford?" Dickon thought the man's tongue must be hung in the middle and could wag at both ends.

"Where? Who knows? Some low tavern, likely.

Drinking and quarreling with his cheap companions whose company he's pleased to keep when he's not carousing with his vile actor friends."

Robin seemed to come to life again. "Do you take care," he said furiously, "how you speak of actors. I'll have. . . ."

It was Dickon who interrupted the tirade this time. "Did Master Marlowe go alone or. . . ."

"How should I know? Do you think I live in his pocket? You could ask the steward except he's off heaven knows where about the place. And now will you be good enough to leave me to my work?"

He didn't wait for an answer but turned again to his scribbling, muttering, "Interruptions, interruptions, interruptions," as Dickon and Robin left the room.

CHAPTER XV

"*The Golden Hind*"

Dickon and Robin, once the courtyard was passed, raced toward the stables and arrived breathless. They did not wait to call for the stableboy but went at once to the stalls and searched among them until they found their own horses, still saddled, to Dickon's unspoken disgust. They led the horses outside and rode back along the bridle path and over the moat at a quiet walk. But once in the broad avenue they put their mounts to a gallop and kept them so all the twelve miles to Deptford.

Robin cursed steadily at first, cursed the crowds in the courtyard who had delayed them and the garrulous scribe in the Great Hall and the steward who was absent from the house. When they had covered the first mile, Dickon said, "Have done, Robin. You'd better save your breath for we'll need whatever strength we have before this day is done."

"How will we find him?" Robin asked. "Where in

all Deptford do we search for one man—or three, if
Kit's still with this Ingram Frizer and his shadow,
whoever that may be."

"Skeres, maybe? I don't like the sound of that,
Robin. I wish Master Blount had seen him in gentler
company. Maybe Mistress Alleyn will know where we
should look?"

"Joan? I doubt it. It's likely she knows even less of
Deptford than I and that's precious little. If it were
London now, I could name you every haunt a theater
man would likely visit. Still we can ask her. And hope.
But I tell you, Dickon, some pricking in my mind
warns me we'd better lose no time."

"Yes," Dickon answered shortly. Like Robin, he was
caught in a dark feeling of immediate doom.

As they rode silently now, side by side, he tried to
understand why he was suddenly so sure the plot was
already afoot. He would take his oath on it a trap was
being laid for Marlowe and would be sprung this day.
Did he feel so because they had been so long in getting
word of Marlowe at Scadbury? Or because the stableboy and the old man had been so violent in their reac-
tions to his name? Or because Master Edward Blount
the stationer had seen him in conversation with a
scoundrel named Ingram Frizer whose last name fitted
what Tom had overheard? That, he thought, was
likely the reason for this growing immediacy of fear.
Were Ingram Frizer and his friends plotting death for
the poet to save their own skins, or were they in league
with some other, some more sinister man or group of

men who feared the knowledge locked in Kit Marlowe's mind, knowledge gained, like as not, upon the Queen's business? No matter. The important thing was to find him and Dickon was increasingly afraid he and Robin were already too late.

Yet, surely, no villains could kill a man without cause in broad daylight in Deptford streets? Surely he and Robin could find Marlowe and warn him. Surely Marlowe himself must be aware of villainy and take care for his own skin. Thus he tried to reassure himself but reassurance would not stick in his mind.

Robin was saying something and Dickon turned his thoughts to listening, hoping for a word of encouragement.

" 'Cut is the branch that might have grown full straight.' He wrote that in *Dr. Faustus*, remember?"

Dickon nodded.

"And he wrote, too, 'Stand still you ever moving spheres of heaven, that time may cease and midnight never come.' The words are for that same Dr. Faustus to speak when he knows his time is over and the devil on the way for him, for you recall he had sold his soul to the devil in return for youth and knowledge. And indeed the words fit well enough in the play. But do you suppose—I'd given no thought to it before—they could also mean Marlowe had some foreknowledge of his own death and is powerless to stop it?"

Dickon felt the skin creep along the back of his neck. If Robin were right. . . . If Marlowe were ordained by some evil fate to die before he was thirty, what good this mad ride to find and warn him? "Nonsense!" he said. "That's nothing but superstitious imagining, Robin."

But he was, himself, not so sure. There were things beyond men's thinking, things that could not be explained by all the logic of all the philosophers in all the schools at Cambridge and Oxford put together. Was not the Bible full of miracles? Was it not generally agreed the stars held influence over the lives of men, as even Queen Elizabeth herself witnessed by the astronomer she kept at her court? And all men knew Gloriana was no stupid, superstitious, unlettered clod, but a wise and learned woman.

He shivered and looked ahead and almost shouted his relief as the first rooftops of Deptford came into sight. Now they could get on with it. Now action would take the place of bootless thinking.

They took the horses to their stable and ran toward the lodgings where they'd left Joan Alleyn and Cicely —how long ago? Two hours? Three? Dickon had lost track of time.

As they came to the churchyard Robin, putting on a great burst of speed, passed Dickon. Dickon grunted thinking Robin would do better to save his breath for the search to come. An extra minute or two now would. . . .

A cry from the churchyard stopped him in midthought. He looked over his shoulder and saw a figure poised on the wall, gesticulating wildly.

Sparrow!

So he'd found them. And caught Dickon Fontayne, alone, in a place where maneuvering would be hard. Dickon looked quickly ahead but could see no sign of Robin. He was, probably, already inside the house. Dickon turned his mind to ways of countering the menace at hand.

The small man on the wall spoke an obscenity and hurled his body toward Dickon, the knife in his hand gleaming cruelly. There was neither time nor space to get away from him. There was only one thing to do.

Dickon hunched his shoulders, head well down between them, and charged the flying figure as if he had been a bull challenging an invasion of his pasture. His head caught Sparrow in mid-flight and the knife flew out of his hand. Sparrow landed on his knees in the dust of the roadway, but, even as Dickon turned, the evil creature was up and coming at him, shouting, "I've got you now, devil's spawn. This time I'll have my revenge and the bauble around your neck—and the girl as well, when I've done with you."

Cicely! Dickon thought and put her out of his mind at once. Only so could he fight this Sparrow and win the fight and protect his girl. He realized the odds were well against him, for Sparrow had found the knife ready to his hand when he'd gone to his knees and was brandishing it at Dickon.

Dickon set his feet more firmly into the roadway and watched his attacker. "Robin!" he called. "To me, Robin!" but he had little hope of making his friend hear him.

Sparrow's wizened face broke into a leer. "Ho!" he said, pausing to wring the final drop of pleasure from having Dickon at his mercy. "Ho! So you'd call on your friend for help. Not so brave this time, I see! And small hope of help. An actor!" Without turning his head he spat in disgust into the road. "Full of soft living and high-sounding words, that tribe. Argh!"

Dickon heard the taunts in silence. He flexed his arms and thanked his stars they were inches longer than Sparrow's. If he could grab his enemy's throat and at the same time kick his legs from under him in the trick Peter had taught him long ago, he had a chance.

Sparrow's face was twisted now with rage. Dickon's silence had infuriated him. He stopped his taunts and squinted his eyes almost shut and Dickon thought *now*. Now he's going to come at me. He breathed deeply and was glad Sparrow was anger-filled, for anger made poor fighters, or so Peter had told him.

Sparrow started toward him and Dickon reached between the short, outstretched arms and got both hands about Sparrow's neck. As he began to squeeze he aimed a kick at Sparrow's ankle and felt the kick connect and heard bone breaking. A lucky hit, he thought.

Sparrow went over backward, dragging Dickon with him. The cry of pain from the broken ankle came as a gurgle between the pressure of Dickon's still squeezing hands.

He had him now, Dickon thought, and anger

against the little man joined fear for Marlowe and he forgot everything except the need to punish this brute of a creature who had planned all manner of evil against Cicely and was, besides, delaying further their search. He banged Sparrow's head into the roadway, again and again and. . . .

"Leave *off*, Dickon." The words, accompanied by strong hands pulling at him, finally penetrated the fog of rage in Dickon's mind. He took his hands away from Sparrow's throat and looked at them as if they belonged to someone else.

"I—I. . . ," Dickon said and Robin thrust him to one side and prodded the gasping body on the ground with his toe.

"You would have killed him, Dickon, if I hadn't missed you at the house and come back for you. Now what's to do?"

Sparrow was groaning. He had dragged himself to a sitting position and was holding his broken ankle in both his hands.

Robin started to lean over, to see what damage had been done, but Sparrow snarled at him, "Go away and leave me alone. I never want to see either of you so long as I live."

"But your ankle," Robin said. "You can't. . . ."

"Go away! Get away from me."

Robin shrugged and turned his back on Sparrow. "Are you hurt, Dickon?" he asked.

Dickon shook his head, dazed still, wondering what had come over him.

"Come along then," Robin said and shook him by the shoulder. "Dickon, come on. We're wasting time!"

"Time?" Dickon said.

"Marlowe, you lackwit."

"M—Marlowe!" Dickon came back into his proper mind with a rush. "Hurry." He turned and looked back at Sparrow and stopped. "But what of him? We can't just leave him there. I think I broke his ankle."

"That you did and almost broke his head as well which would have been no more than he deserved. Except it would have got us into the clutches of the constables, which we have no time for. Don't fret over him. He wants no help from us. He'll manage well enough, I'll warrant. And he's learned his lesson. He'll not trouble you again. Or Cicely."

"His friends?" Dickon muttered.

"He's got no friends," Robin said. "If he had he'd never have come for you alone. I know his kind. Come, I had only just roused the little maidservant when I missed you and came back to find you."

They went back to the house and found the maid waiting for them. She stared at Dickon's disheveled clothes but she made no comment upon them. Robin went past her and was already at the foot of the stairs when she said, "If it's Mistress Alleyn and the strange young lady you seek, they're not here."

Robin swore and Dickon, holding impatience upon a tight rein, asked, "Where are they? Where have they gone?"

"They didn't say, Master." The little maid smiled

up at him, her eyes twinkling with mischief. "But I'd guess they are about and about at the draper's and the mantuamakers and the milliner's, for they were agog with plans for a wardrobe for the young lady and I did wish I stood in her shoes!"

Robin was as woebegone as if he'd heard of a death in his family. "Devil take all women," he said. "We'll never find them, bustling about from shop to shop and who's to say where and how many? So now what's to do?"

"Now," Dickon said sharply, "we start our search." With a quick word of thanks to the girl he turned again into the cobbled street. Robin followed him and they stood for a moment not knowing where to begin.

Dickon said, "Robin, you must have heard, at least, something of the habits of Christopher Marlowe. Where would he go to pass a time of idleness in Deptford?" He held up his hand as Robin started to answer. "No. Wait a moment. I think we'd better consider the worst chance and assume he is not alone but accompanied by two men—at least two, maybe more if they should have been joined by that Robert Poley we heard of—men we know to be very rascals. So where would three or four go in this town?"

"Alone or with any number of companions I'd guess Kit Marlowe would go to a tavern, for he loves his ale and his talk and taverns are fine places for both," Robin answered.

"So. Which tavern?"

"The saints alone would know. There must be dozens in Deptford. I can't even say of a surety they'd go to the best, for it's said Kit cares little in what surroundings he drinks so long as there are people to argue with."

"Then we'll have to search them all," Dickon declared.

"Dickon! Do you know what you propose? That would likely take us days. We don't even know where to begin!"

"Do you have a better thought?"

"No."

"Then we'll begin where the town begins and search out every tavern sign till it ends. And we'll not think beyond this day for we can only do what we can do."

They started at the first tavern they had passed as they came from Scadbury. Their looking was slow work. Each lane and byway had to be tramped, their feet often mired in the filthy ditches because their eyes were, of necessity, on the lookout for the creaking signs that showed a unicorn or a mermaid, a greyhound or a golden lion or one of the score of other creatures that designated drinking places. Once they discovered a sign, they went in and waited for their eyes to adjust to the dim light before they moved from table to table peering into each face so that Robin could be sure no one there was, in fact, Christopher Marlowe. Occasionally they found an empty tavern, the host standing forlorn and sullen behind his bar. But usually the rooms were crowded with men of all conditions, their businesses disorganized or ruined by the long months of plague, making do with ale to pass the empty hours.

All day they searched and found no sign of Marlowe or of the men they thought might be with him. Once, tired and hot, they took time to drink a draft of ale. For a small while, then, they found heart but the false cheer brought by the brew was soon gone. They had eaten no food since early morning when, late in the afternoon, the sky darkened and thunder ran along the clouds settling over London. They had been walking on a cobbled street that led to the river and, as they came near its end, they saw a ship-of-war, or so it seemed, huddled close against the dockside. Her sails were tight-furled and her ratlines snapped in the rising storm winds.

"Look!" Dickon, roused from the fog of weariness that held him, took Robin's arm and pointed. "Why is a great warship docked here instead of harbored on the coast? Poor thing. It looks for all the world like some great netted bird."

Robin shook himself into awareness of his surroundings. "Why indeed? There's a name upon her bow. *The Golden Hind.* That's Drake's ship. Ah, I remember now. I did hear the ship is forever anchored here and is become a tavern." His voice quickened with excitement. "It may be this is the very place we seek. It would surely please the love of far places that walks always with Kit Marlowe to take his ale in a ship that has sailed right around the world."

Dickon caught the excitement and, finding new

strength in their tired legs, they ran the remaining way to the dockside as lightning cracked over Thames water and the first great drops of the early summer storm wet their shoulders.

A blare of noise stunned their ears as they opened the door upon a room filled with light from two-score lanterns fixed to the wall of what had been the captain's cabin. They stood just within the door adjusting their senses to yet another place where Marlowe might be sitting among the crowd.

The ship, rocking a little as the Thames rose and fell with the incoming tide, stank of old wine and sweat and burning oil mixed with the pipes of tobacco Walter Raleigh had made popular when English ships had brought back the weed from the new-found lands across the western ocean. Small tables, their bare boards scrubbed white, were set about the room. Each bore a thick candle that flared when the door was opened and dropped its grease and added the odor of tallow to the general musty smell. Most of the chairs about the tables were filled with men, many of them half-drunken, some talking pleasantly, some quarreling, some singing.

Dickon, for the first time in this long day, swore and wished he'd never heard of Christopher Marlowe. He was sick of the sound and the smell of taverns. He lifted his aching shoulders and prepared for the twentieth time to make a circuit of a room, sure in his mind this one would be as fruitless as the rest.

CHAPTER XVI

End of a Quest

"Marlowe is dead!"

The words shouted from the door crashed through Dickon's head, echoed and re-echoed in the room suddenly as silent as midnight. The babel had stopped. The crowds of noisy men sat as if they were figures carved on a roodscreen, their movements as stilled as their tongues.

"Kit Marlowe is dead, I say."

Dickon shook his head a little, willing himself not to believe what he heard; trying to pursuade himself this was no more than the imagining of his tired brain.

"Dickon!" Robin's voice in his ear was tight with feeling. "Dickon, do you hear? Marlowe is dead! Kit Marlowe is dead and we—we have failed. We are too late."

So, the fatal words were not in his tired mind, Dickon thought as the tavern exploded again into loud, excited cries.

"WHAT?"

"What's that you're saying? Dead? Marlowe dead? But he can't be. I saw him myself only this morning. He. . . ."

"And may he rot in hell! Brawler! Schemer! Atheist! Papist! I. . . ."

"You can't have it both ways, friend. Not *both* atheist and papist." This was a quiet voice that cut under the noise and stilled it for a moment. But only for a moment.

"He was the greatest poet of our time. Do you remember the lines in. . . ?"

"And likely the greatest lover of England."

"Atheist! Kit Marlowe an atheist? Who says it?"

"I. I say it who had it from. . . ."

"Then you shall answer to me who say you lie. Out sword! Have at you then!

"GENTLEMEN!" This voice topped them all. "Put up your swords. I'll have no fighting here. Put them up, I say, or I'll call the watch. That's better. Now if you will hold your rattling tongues, we can hear this ill news it has pleased Wat Smith to bring us."

A man dressed in a leather apron over greasy, baggy pants and a dirty shirt of coarse brown linen was being hoisted upon a table. The shouting quieted to a mumble that buzzed in the room like bees when their hive is threatened. As the landlord—he of the mighty voice —spoke, even the buzzing ceased.

"Now, Wat Smith," the landlord said, "tell us the whole of it and tell it true, mind."

"Master Marlowe—" Wat Smith began and got no further.

"*Master* Marlowe indeed," a man cried out from a table along the back wall, "that low-born, devil-raising, son of a. . . ."

"Hus-s-sh." The word hissed from many throats at once, diminishing like the waves receding from the shore at low tide, and the man was still.

Wat Smith, aware suddenly that every mind in the room awaited his words, coughed and shuffled his feet on the table.

"Well, Wat?" the landlord said. "Speak up man, speak up. There's no one here will harm you but none of us wants to wait the night through to hear your tale."

"He's dead," Wat Smith said. He stuttered a little at first but after a few words he forgot his uncertainty in the unaccustomed glory of being the center of attention. "Kit Marlowe is, in very truth, as dead as mortal man can be."

"How?"

"When?"

"Where?"

The questions came shooting at him like arrows at the butts.

"Just now," Wat Smith said. He coughed again, then rushed on. "And this is the way of it. This Marlowe, being required by the council to keep himself close at hand to wait upon the pleasures of their lordships, was staying the while at Scadbury Manor with his friend

and patron, Master Thomas Walsingham, he that
is. . . ."

Someone called out, "Get on with it, can't you?"

Wat gulped and reddened and went on. "Yes. As I
was saying, this Marlowe was staying at Scadbury for
he fears the plague like any mortal man and London is
foul with it now."

"We know that. Give us the gist of it!"

Wat held up his hand. "Do you listen, then, and let
me say my say. This day, in the morning, this Marlowe
went with three others to Eleanor Bull's tavern hard
by. . . ."

"Their names! Give us the names of the others."

"Their names?" Wat Smith sounded surprised, as if
everyone should know this simple thing. "Why their
names are Robert Poley and Ingram Frizer and Nicholas Skeres, and they are taken up and bound over to
wait their trial for murder—though they say it was an
accident, this killing."

Dickon groaned and Robin said, "Hush!"

"They were, all the four of them, at this house of
Mistress Bull's all the day, in a private room talking
and drinking strong ale. They walked a little in the
garden toward sunset, for it was hot, and then went in
again to sup. And after supper there was a quarrel, no
man will say what about, and this Marlowe, sitting
upon a bench between two of his companions, was
stabbed above the eye by this Frizer and died in-
stanter. And all this I had from Giles, the potboy, and
it's true as I stand here to tell it."

So, Dickon thought amid the hubbub that followed Smith's words, it was over. They had failed and he felt as if some dire thing had come out of the sky and hit him so hard a blow he could scarcely breathe. He knew now that what had begun as a favor promised to his dying brother had become a thing so close to him it seemed a very part of his life. Christopher Marlowe was dead and Tom was dead and he, Dickon Fontayne, wished he were dead himself. He wanted to get up and run. Run anywhere, so long as it was away from this room and this little man who had brought a world of sorrow and regret tumbling about his ears. He half rose and Robin pulled him back.

"Wait!" Robin commanded and Dickon sank back into his chair, too drained to do more than obey. He sat very still, the core of him filled with despair and pity, while the top of his mind took idle note of the room and its occupants.

After a moment a man seated alone at a table near them rose and looked about him. He was a young man, no more than thirty, soberly dressed, with a quiet manner. His eyes, deepset above a tuft of moustache and a beard cut in the style made popular by the Dutch painter Van Dyke, searched the room, seeming to judge each man there with understanding and compassion and justice. Slowly he picked up a traveling cape from the back of his chair and threw it about his shoulders with a graceful gesture. He said, softly, but in a voice that seemed to accuse each man who had spoken since Wat Smith had spread abroad his news.

"That was a great reckoning in a little room. What a loss is England's!"

He stood a moment more, observing them all, judging them all, in a sense, accusing them all before he walked with grace and dignity to the door that led onto the deck of The Golden Hind. As he passed, Dickon heard one man whisper to another, "Who was that?" and the reply, "Will Shakespeare of Stratford. Mark him well. All England will know him for his playmaking before many years have passed, or I'm no judge."

Robin tugged at Dickon's sleeve. "Dickon," he whispered and there was that in his voice that said he couldn't bear any more. "Dickon, let us go from this place."

They went, half stumbling, through the door and out upon the deck and down the gangplank of Drake's ship and into the waterside lane. The rain had slackened to a fine drizzle as they moved in streets darkened by houses whose upper stories all but met above their heads. Once, as they walked, not talking, a man, slinking from the deepest shadows close to the walls, made to come toward them, his eyes gleaming with malice and greed. They didn't hear him mutter, "Proper gulls," nor see the stout club that threatened them. But the club never fell for there was something in the dejection of the two bowed figures that stopped the footpad in his tracks. He made the sign against evil and withdrew once more into the deepest shadows.

After a while, Robin said, "He's dead. Our playmaker is dead. Oh, why weren't we more diligent in our search?"

The words, underlining all he had himself been thinking seemed to drive the chill rain right through Dickon's body. He said, "Peace, Robin," and walked on again in silence.

But in that silence he seemed to hear a voice which said, "*Che sera, sera.* What will be, will be. Lift up your mind to the stars and waste no time in moaning."

The words were so clear in his mind, he almost thought Christopher Marlowe himself must be beside him, with his philosophy of accepting things as they came without fuss or worry. Dickon straightened his shoulders and lifted his head. They had failed to find Marlowe and warn him. So much was true, though they had not failed of their own fault. Maybe, in very truth, this death had been written in the stars since time began.

But what of the men who had killed Marlowe? Would they be properly punished for their act? Shouldn't he and Robin go back, go to the magistrate and tell him all they knew of the scoundrels who had spent a day with Marlowe as his friends, knowing in their hearts they would kill him at its end?

"Dickon," Robin said as if they two were of one single mind. "Let's go back and tell the magistrate all we know of this affair.

Dickon didn't answer him at once and Robin took his arm and shook it.

"I hear you, Robin," Dickon said. "I was taking a little time to consider. But, faith, I think it would do no good. What can we tell them? That a fever-ridden man heard in Dover what he thought to be a plot against his friend's life? 'Who plotted?' the magistrate would ask. And 'Who were these plotters? What were their names?' And 'What was the plot? Was Mistress Eleanor Bull mentioned? When was the plot to take place?' So —to all these questions we can only hang our heads and answer 'I don't know.' "

"But we have those three names John Howland gave us. And one of them—or all of them—killed Marlowe. And we know Tom heard a part of one of those names spoken at Dover. That would point to a plot, planned in advance, and it would prove this day's evil work was no accident."

"And don't you know Poley and Frizer and Skeres would swear, separately and together, they were not in Dover at the time, had not been in Dover for years. And bring rascals in scores to prove their lie."

"But Dickon, we could tell how Sparrow tried to kill you at Oxford and again this day."

"You're not thinking, Robin. What has that to do with Christopher Marlowe? Besides, who can say our three men were the *real* murderers? Who can say they were not set to it by men in high places who fear for their own skins? What chance would we have against the word of such a man as Thomas Walsingham? No, I'm not accusing him. But there may be men of his ilk who have cause to fear what Christopher Marlowe held in his mind."

"But we can't just go about our own affairs and do nothing."

"We can. We will. We must, Robin. Don't you know I'm as filled with horror as you at this fell deed? I feel as if my own life has been diminished by Marlowe's death. But consider, Robin, and consider well. There's more, much more in this murder than we can fathom. I'm sure of it. It may even be a matter that somehow touches the State itself, or the Queen, though I can't see just how. For don't forget, if your Ned Alleyn is right, Christopher Marlowe had been but lately upon the Queen's business. It's not for us to meddle in such matters. No. Marlowe is dead. And, much as I'd like to see his murderers punished, such punishment will not bring him back. Alas! And our meddling might stir up such a nest of hornets as would wreck some plans we cannot know of."

Robin said slowly, "It still doesn't seem quite—quite just somehow. But I suppose you're right."

They had stopped, regardless of the rain, while they talked. Now Robin let his shoulders sink forward as if, once he'd spoken what was in his mind, he was free again to attend to his grief.

"We'd better go on," Dickon said, "and tell Mistress Joan and Cicely before rumor runs ahead of us."

"Come, Robin," he added sharply when Robin didn't move. "There'll be time enough, for both of us, for grieving."

He tugged at Robin's arm and got him moving like, Dickon thought, the walking dead. But a person must

go on living and thinking and planning. No matter
what happened. As long as he was alive. He was sure
Kit Marlowe would have it so. He thought Marlowe
would say death must come to all men, but while you
lived you had an obligation to life; an obligation to use
your mind and heart to the fullest of their powers; an
obligation not to let grief destroy you; an obligation to
let nothing get in the way of seeking the truth. Likely
Robin would never see it so. Robin was a doer, not a
thinker. But he was a good friend for all that.

Dickon said, "Lift up your heart, Robin, and set reasonable bounds to sorrow. For so you can best honor
Christopher Marlowe."

Robin gave him no answer and they came at last to
the house by the church and knocked. Cicely herself
let them in and when she saw them she cried out,
sounding angry in her relief they were come back after
all these hours of waiting, unharmed.

"Where have you been? Do you know the hour?
Mistress Joan and I—we've been half-dead with
worry."

When neither of them answered, she looked at them
more closely and saw their white, unhappy faces and
said, "What is it? What's happened, Dickon?"

He put an arm about her and pulled her close to
him and kissed her. Robin left them, walking wearily
as an old man up the stairs to Joan Alleyn. Dickon
closed the door and, when Cicely would have gone
after Robin, held her back. "Best leave him to Mistress
Joan, my love. He's sick with sorrow—and indeed so

am I. Marlowe is dead, silenced forever in a fight, so it's said, with those men we know of, Robert Poley and Nicholas Skeres and Ingram Frizer."

"Oh, Dickon," she said. "You came too late."

"Too late," he echoed and told her of their long day's searching and of its end. "So now it's over," he finished, "and I feel limp as an empty sack and full of sadness. And," he found to his surprise, as the words came out in spite of himself, he could not so easily be rid of the burden of guilt, "and guilty that we did not come in time."

She spoke sharply, rebuking him, "That is a matter for laughter! You must, in truth, be worn out with your seeking to think such things. Use your head. Even if you'd found your man at Scadbury and given him warning, it would, likely, have done no good. For all men say he was hard of head and would listen to no wisdom but his own. No. Don't interrupt me. You yourself said your Marlowe was not one to shun danger, not even to save his own life. It's over, Dickon. OVER. You did what you could. What's done is done and the past is over. And we have much to plan for the future—our future, together. Don't let your mind keep lingering and fretting over what can't be helped."

Dickon looked at her and saw her eyes shining with hope for their future and love for him. She was right, of course. He remembered hearing one of the philosophers at Cambridge who had, he thought, been quoting another, say, "You can't step twice into the same stream." For, the philosopher had explained, the flowing water changed from second to second and never remains the same. So be it. Robin would give himself over to grief for his lost playmaker for a while yet. But his grieving wouldn't bring Marlowe back to life. And, in a little time, Robin would recover and, likely, forget.

For himself, well he too would grieve—maybe a little, even to the end of his life—for an ideal lost. But now—now he would go back to Scadbury tomorrow and find Master Edward Blount, the stationer and printer, and ask for work as a scrivener until the plague was gone and the playhouses opened again. Then, with Ned Alleyn's help, he would begin to live a new life.

He kissed Cicely again and took her hand and started toward the crooked stairs that led up to Joan Alleyn's rooms. The ways of his life would, likely, be as crooked as that stairway. There would be other failures, other disappointments, other sorrows. But it wouldn't matter. It was the manner of your living and thinking that was important. That he had learned from the plays of Christopher Marlowe and no man could take that away from him. It had taken time and a tragedy at the end for the message to come plain and clear in his mind. Now, please God, he could go where his life would take him. Nor would he quarrel if the path were not always easy or the way straight. That would signify nothing. Not so long as he held to the truth.

Afterword

CHRISTOPHER MARLOWE, first of the great sixteenth-century playwrights and contemporary of William Shakespeare, was also a spy for Queen Elizabeth during the troubled times of her reign when Spain and the Pope were plotting to recover England for Catholicism. Marlowe was a man about whom people had strong feelings. He was either well loved or well hated. We don't know a great deal about him, except what we know of his plays. He was born in Canterbury where his father was a leather worker and a man of some importance in the community. Young Christopher was educated at the Cathedral School in Canterbury and later at Cambridge. He was a spy for Queen Elizabeth I's minister, Sir Francis Walsingham. He went to London when he had completed his education and wrote six plays and two poems which were popular with readers and playgoers alike. He was the first English playwright to use blank verse for his plays. He was killed in Eleanor Bull's tavern by Ingram Frizer, Nicholas Skeres, and Robert Poley. Though they were cleared of the charge of murder, the accounts of Marlowe's death point clearly to premeditation. So far no one has been able to discover certainly why he was killed but many authorities today seem to agree his death was a result, in some manner, of his undercover work.

NED ALLEYN (pronounced A-*lain*) was a leading actor in the Elizabethan theater. He brought to life upon the stage all of Marlowe's characters, most notably Tamburlaine, Edward II, and Dr. Faustus. He made a fortune for himself and his beloved wife, Joan, to whom he wrote charming letters whenever he was "on the road." He really did call her his "mouse."

THOMAS WALSINGHAM was a cousin of SIR FRANCIS WALSINGHAM, Queen Elizabeth's spymaster. Francis Walsingham died in 1590, three years before Marlowe, but his system of spying continued to be used for many years after his death. Thomas Walsingham did live at Scadbury Manor and was a patron to Marlowe among many others.

EDWARD BLOUNT was a stationer and printer, or in modern terms, a book publisher. He was a friend of Christopher Marlowe's and published the first, incomplete version of *Hero and Leander*, just as Marlowe had left it when he was killed. A later version, "completed" by one of Marlowe's friends, appeared later.

SKERES, FRIZER, and POLEY, the men responsible for Marlowe's death, lived on the edge of what we should today call the underworld. Their wits and their daggers were for hire and they had few scruples about what they did. Frizer was Thomas Walsingham's "man"—i.e., under his protection and, to some extent, financed by him as was the custom in those days. Skeres seems to have been a very low character, a hanger-on of Frizer's. Robert Poley, the most sinister of the three, was a known spy of Sir Francis Walsingham's. But he was ready to turn his coat whenever he was offered more money and he never cared what means he used to gain his ends. Today we should call him a double agent.

The other leading characters in the book are imaginary.

The paintings of American Indians that hung upon the walls of Scadbury Manor, Thomas Walsingham's home, were done by John White who accompanied Sir Walter Raleigh's settlers to Roanoke Island in 1588, though White did not stay with them to be lost forever in the New World. The paintings now hang in the British Museum.

There is in fact an oak tree, still standing on the grounds of Scadbury Manor, where the initials CM are cut, vertically, deep into the bark. The letters are now moss-covered but still readable. No man can say they were cut there by Christopher Marlowe, but no man can say they were not, and the legend that he did indeed cut them persists in the neighborhood.

The title for this book comes from Shakespeare's play *As You Like It,* and it is generally believed to refer to Marlowe's death. It is interesting to remember that Shakespeare was born in the same year as Marlowe, though Shakespeare was only just beginning the full tide of his writing career when Marlowe died. It is also interesting to speculate what strides Marlowe might have made in his playwriting if he had not been killed. On the other hand, he may well have moved on to other things and written no more plays. A list of his works is given below:

PLAYS:	*Tamburlaine*	1587 (or 1588)
	Dido, Queen of Carthage	1587
	Massacre at Paris	1589
	The Jew of Malta	1590
	Edward II	1592
	The Tragical History of Dr. Faustus	1593
POEMS:	*The Passionate Shepherd to His Love*	
	Hero and Leander	

Glossary

Assizes: Courts of justice.

Atheist: Although atheist meant the same thing in the sixteenth century that it means today, it had a very different impact on the ordinary people of the period. To call a man an atheist at that time was the equivalent of calling him a traitor—or, in today's terms, perhaps, calling him a communist or soviet agent.

Camelbird: Sixteenth-century name for the ostrich.

Coiner: Counterfeiter.

Cry of players: A collective noun used for a troupe of actors. Such troupes, in the sixteenth century, were often sponsored by a great lord and called after his name, e.g., "The Lord Admiral's Men" or "Lord Strange's Men." In normal times these troupes—or at least the best of them—played on the London stages during the winter and traveled about the countryside during the summer months playing at innyards in the larger towns and in university towns. In 1592–1593 the London playhouses were closed because of the plague and the traveling companies of actors were driven into the provinces, where some of them had to be disbanded for lack of funds.

Ewer: A pitcher with a wide spout.

Farthing: A coin equal to the fourth part of an English penny or (in our money) about half a cent.

Four elements: These were blood, phlegm, choler, and black choler. According to sixteenth-century thinking, everybody was made up of these elements in differing proportions and the extent to which one element or humor predominated determined the character of the individual.

Gloriana: One of the names for Queen Elizabeth I.

Leeches: Doctors; also small animals used to suck the blood of ill people. Bloodletting was one of the chief treatments for any and all ailments in the sixteenth century—so much so that the name of the little animals used to cleanse the body came to be the recognized name for doctor.

Point-device: Perfectly correct, especially in dress.

Reckoning: Bill for food or drink or lodging.

Roodscreen: A wooden screen supporting a cross at the entrance to the part of the church that holds the altar or communion table.